C000097280

TORRES DEL PAINE

TORRES DEL PAINE

DAVID D. WALKER

Copyright © 2021 David D Walker

The moral right of the author has been asserted.

Apart from any fair dealing for the purposes of research or private study,
or criticism or review, as permitted under the Copyright, Designs and Patents
Act 1988, this publication may only be reproduced, stored or transmitted, in
any form or by any means, with the prior permission in writing of the
publishers, or in the case of reprographic reproduction in accordance with
the terms of licences issued by the Copyright Licensing Agency. Enquiries
concerning reproduction outside those terms should be sent to the publishers.

All characters in this story – other than the obvious historical figures – are fictitious
and any resemblance to real persons, living or dead, is purely coincidental.

Matador
9 Priory Business Park,
Wistow Road, Kibworth Beauchamp,
Leicestershire. LE8 0RX
Tel: 0116 279 2299
Email: books@troubador.co.uk
Web: www.troubador.co.uk/matador
Twitter: @matadorbooks

ISBN 978 1800461 741

British Library Cataloguing in Publication Data.
A catalogue record for this book is available from the British Library.

Typeset in 11pt Adobe Garamond Pro by Troubador Publishing Ltd, Leicester, UK

Matador is an imprint of Troubador Publishing Ltd

For Janet, Rachel and Nichola
My travelling companions through life and around the world

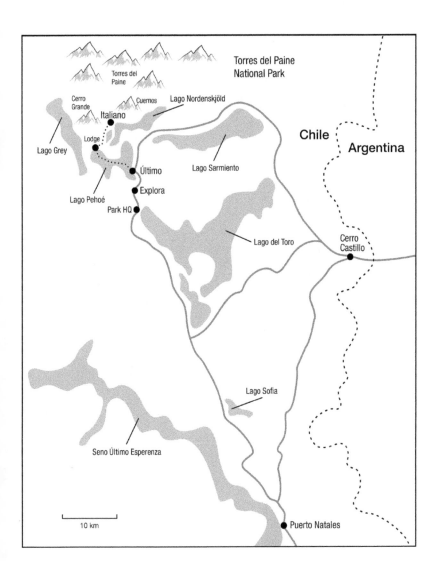

PROLOGUE

It was no way for a US senator to die, sitting with his pants around his ankles.

It was no place for a US senator to die – literally in a foreign shithole.

The structure around him swayed in the gale, and the wind whistled through the knotholes and cracks in the thin wood planking. Cold air poured through the hole behind his neck and swirled round his uncovered shins. The dreadful smell emanating from between his legs was overpowering, despite the unwanted ventilation. He felt a band tightening around his heart, his mouth and throat burned, his bowels emptied into the stench below, and he thought that his head was about to explode. Sweat poured off his brow and ran into his eyes, joining tears, which in turn coalesced with the green mucus slime emanating from his nose. He grabbed his neck in an attempt to stop the throbbing pain there and squeezed hard.

This couldn't be happening to him.

This shouldn't be happening to him.

He was a senator – chosen by the people.

He was a war hero.

He was a somebody.

He was going to be President of the United States, goddammit.

He opened his mouth to scream, but no sound emerged.

Then, for Dwayne Towers, all went black.

CHAPTER 1

Nacho sat with his feet on the desk, leaning back in his office chair. As he glanced up from his reading and looked past his jean-clad legs and Converse trainers, he could see raindrops migrating horizontally from right to left across his window, driven by the furious wind outside. Beyond the rattling windows, he could just make out the indistinct outlines of Puerto Natales, including the faint shape of the town's cathedral tower, the looming post office on the far side of the Plaza des Armas, and the coloured roofs of houses beyond.

He put down *Las Últimas Noticias*, having read the tabloid's sports pages, pretending to himself that he hadn't really scanned the salacious, sexy gossip columns as well. He was gratified to see that his football club, Universidad de Chile, was doing better this season than last, and already had a couple of good wins under their belt. Last year he'd suffered the angst of relegation, and it had only been avoided when the league was suspended due to the protests that had started in October.

Nacho picked up *El Mercurio* to continue his browsing. The newspaper was a little conservative for his taste, but it was the heavyweight of the Chilean press. It was also well-connected to the government, and so always worth a read. The front page was full of the usual political bickering on how to solve the issues raised during the protests. From what he had read, and seen on the television news, the riots were getting less frequent and limited in their geography, but there was still a hard core of protesters. He thought the majority had been bought off for now by the government's promise of a referendum in April, only two months away. The vote was to be on a new constitution which would allegedly address the issues being raised on social inequality, escalating living costs, and the privatisation of state-owned enterprises. Nacho shared the scepticism within the general population about the political classes. From an article he'd read previously in *El Mercurio*, it seemed to him that this was not unique to Chile, and quite widespread with examples cited in America, Britain, and much of Europe. France had something called the *Gilets Jaune* movement, whose discontent sounded quite aligned with Chile's home-grown protesters. Even in Australia, the prime minister had been lambasted by his electorate for committing the major faux pas of holidaying while his country burned in widespread bush fires.

In other news, he read about a new disease in China called coronavirus, centred on somewhere called Wuhan, but with cases now being reported internationally. There seemed to be worries that it could spread like the earlier SARS epidemic or the Spanish flu of 1918. It sounded serious, but far, far away.

The Swedish teenager, Greta Thunberg, was warning anybody who would listen about global warming. Unfortunately, most of the politicians didn't seem to be doing much listening. Nacho was convinced that the effect was real and Chile was certainly experiencing more extreme weather, with a drought in the central valleys, home to much of the country's agriculture and vineyards, a particular concern. *How could anyone with half a brain not see it?* Nacho wondered. *Then again*, he thought, *these people avoiding the topic are Chilean politicians.* From his reading, they seemed keen that the whole topic be swept under the carpet after the embarrassment of cancelling the UN's Climate Conference in Santiago because of the riots.

Reading on, he learned from *El Mercurio*'s sports pages that Alexis didn't seem to be doing any better at Inter Milan than he had at Manchester United. The Chilean star appeared to have gone off the boil. *What a pity*, thought Nacho, for the forward had been a great player for Chile and was one of Nacho's favourites.

Nacho felt slightly sleepy after his lunch of a burger washed down by a couple of own-brewed craft beers in Baguale's Pub along the street from the police station. He'd have to be sure that this didn't become a habit. He'd put on a couple of kilos recently and although his 1.8-metre frame could just about handle it, he couldn't afford a new wardrobe, and he didn't want to make himself less attractive to the opposite sex. He decided to take a short nap and save reading *The Clinic,* his favourite satirical newspaper, until later.

Just as he started to doze off, the phone on his desk rang, startling him. Nacho wondered what it would be about. A cat up a tree? A drunk fallen into the harbour? Since his reassignment to Patagonia from Santiago, he'd had only one murder to deal with. It had been an open-and-shut case, a crime of passion, where a sailor, arriving off the Navimag coastal ferry from Puerto Montt, had come home early and found his wife in bed with his best friend. A kitchen knife covered in the cuckold's fingerprints was recovered at the scene, and the murderer himself was found an hour later in one of the waterfront bars slumped in a puddle of spilled beer. All in all, it was a lot simpler and less murky than his last case in the capital with its political overtones. Those overtones had resulted in his transfer to the PDI's station in Puerto Natales in Última Esperanza Province in the southernmost reaches of Chile. The province billed itself as "The End of the World".

'Hello, Inspector Ignatius Hernández, Investigations Police, the PDI, speaking. How can I help you?'

'Please wait, I have the Director General on the line for you,' said a well-spoken female voice.

'Is that Hernández in Puerto Natales?' said a gruff voice in Nacho's ear. Nacho laughed.

'Very good, Pablo, you sound just like the old bastard himself. If I didn't know your old tricks, I could almost have fallen for it!'

'I'm sorry to disappoint you, Hernández, but this is in fact the "old bastard" himself calling from PDI Headquarters in Santiago, and if you don't listen to what I've got to say with 100 per cent of your attention, I'll have you busted to *aspirante* and sent even further away to Puerto Williams. Do you hear me, Hernández?'

The voice had a tone of menace and Nacho quickly concluded that he was, for some reason, speaking to the DG of the Investigations Police, Chile's most senior civil policeman.

'Yes, sir. Sorry, sir.'

'I understand from your previous bosses here at HQ that you were one of our best up-and-coming detectives in the Homicide Brigade.'

'Thank you, sir.'

'I also understand from them that's why you made inspector so quickly.'

'Kind of them to say so, sir.'

'Well, for your information, it was for that reason that I personally intervened to have you sent to Puerto Natales to protect you from political forces at the Ministry. There were those at La Moneda who were uncomfortable with your investigation into the death of one of the protest leaders. They didn't like your conclusion that a senior Carabineros' officer might be involved.'

Nacho's hopes began to rise. *Maybe I'm being recalled to Santiago and my exile is being terminated*, he thought. His hopes were dashed by the DG's next sentence.

'When things have cooled down in the future, you'll be brought back here, but in the meantime, I have a delicate, important, and indeed, urgent, task for you.'

'I'm at your disposal, sir,' said Nacho, taking his feet off the desk and sitting upright in his chair.

'An American senator has died in the Torres del Paine National Park. A certain Dwayne Towers. He was quite old, and he probably

4

died of natural causes on a hike, but, unfortunately, a journalist who is present in the park has pre-empted any controlled news of the Senator's demise by tweeting that he died in "suspicious circumstances". CNN and the other news channels have picked it up and it's trending on Twitter. Apparently, he was a great supporter of President Trump. As a result of all this, the American Embassy here in Santiago is about to send a planeload of FBI, CIA, and, for all I know, NYPD, CSI, and the US Marines, down your way to find out what happened. The press will be hot on their heels. You can expect CNN and Fox News to be right behind them. However, we will not have foreigners trampling across our jurisdiction! Your job is to get your ass up to the park as quick as you can and find out if there is anything at all suspicious about the Senator's death.'

'Right, sir, I'll get up there first thing tomorrow,' said Nacho, looking out of the window once more at the appalling weather.

'Perhaps I didn't make myself clear, Inspector Hernández?' said the DG, emphasising Nacho's much lower rank. 'I said as quick as you can, as in "as soon as possible", as in "right now", Hernández!' The DG's voice had risen higher and louder as this sentence had progressed and he had veritably roared the word "now".

'I understand, sir. I'm just wondering why me? Shouldn't someone more senior from Punta Arenas address this?'

'As I said earlier, you've worked in homicide, and while I'm praying this isn't one, I need to be seen to send someone competent to hold the fort and gather any evidence. Also, I see from your file that you're fluent in English. Most of the witnesses will no doubt be English speakers as the Senator was staying at the Último Hotel. Not many Chileans can afford to stay there. That's where you're to go this afternoon, as in "immediately". Do you finally get it?'

'Yes, sir. And will you let the Prosecutor's Office know?'

'There's no need for the Prosecutor's Office for now. We don't even know if a crime's been committed yet, do we? We'll cross that bridge when we come to it. In the meantime, I'll square everything away with your boss down there while you get up to Torres del Paine.'

'And what about the Carabineros, sir?'

'What about them?'

'Should I involve them to help with legwork?'

'No, you should not! We don't want those clodhoppers involved. They have about as much tact as a bull in a china shop. This is far too sensitive for them.'

'And should I order up our forensics team from Punto Arenas?'

'No need. We don't know what we're dealing with yet. Now get going, Hernández. Only communicate on this matter directly to me. Do you understand? I think you have twenty-four hours, maybe forty-eight hours before the US Cavalry arrive to interfere, depending on the weather. I gather it's quite breezy down there right now?'

'Yes, you could say that, sir,' replied Nacho, smiling at the DG's understatement.

'Nevertheless, I need you to go there and find out what happened before the Americans get there.'

'Yes, sir. I'll be there by this evening.'

'That's all. Dismissed, Hernández.'

After he put the phone down, Nacho looked out of the window again at the charcoal-grey sky and the blurred silhouette of the town. The image was accompanied by a soundtrack of howling wind and the machine gun-like rattle of rain on glass. *The trouble with a Patagonian summer*, he thought, *is that it's the windiest season.* Nacho knew that although not a particularly rainy period, squalls like the one outside were frequent, visibility for driving was often poor, and road-holding in sudden gusts a problem. Still, orders were orders.

Guiltily, Nacho hoped it was indeed a suspicious death to compensate for the sheer boredom of his recent existence. In Santiago he had always been busy, and, although the murder rate in Chile overall wasn't high by international standards, with a population of over five million in the capital, there had always been an interesting case to work on.

Furthermore, the reason for his exclusion to Patagonia still rankled. While Nacho agreed with the October protesters about many things, as a civilian police officer he felt people should use their vote and not violence to achieve their political aims. Unfortunately, with politicians held in low esteem by most of his countrymen, the people had taken to the streets to try to change things for themselves. The troubles had ultimately spiralled out of control with 12,000 protesters and 1,900 Carabineros injured. There had been accusations of torture, strip searches, and even rape by the Carabineros and the military as they'd tried to control the situation, but often abused human rights along the way. A state of emergency and curfews had been imposed. Rubber bullets, tear gas, and shotguns had been used against the protesters and nearly thirty people had died.

One of those deaths had not been on the street, but at an activist's home and Nacho had investigated at a prosecutor's direction. He'd found a trail that led to a clandestine group of Carabineros officers who had decided to take the law into their own hands. This rogue element, no doubt believing they were patriots, had simply gone too far. Nacho felt he had gathered enough evidence to have one of the most senior culprits arrested when his investigation had been shut down. Although personally ready to fight this apparent abuse of power, he had been warned off by his father, who had lost a brother to the fascist Pinochet regime twenty years previously. His father said he couldn't bear having another member of his family become a "disappeared". In the same month, President Piñera had instigated reforms with respect to police conduct towards the protesters. Respecting his father, and hoping the President would deliver, Nacho had backed off and agreed to be sent down for a period to Puerto Natales and off the radar of any forces wishing him or his family ill will.

As it turned out, the timing was fine. His girlfriend, Maria, had split from him saying she could no longer go out with a member of the reactionary forces. Maria was quite left wing, a lecturer at the Universidad Católica, and an ardent protester. They had met at university where they had both studied economics. While she had carried on in academia, he had joined the PDI with a burning ambition to root out financial corruption in the country. As part of his police training, he had been assigned for a period to the Homicide Brigade and found out that he was actually quite good at solving murders. He had been drawn into that vocation; his corruption busting put on hold. This was another sore point with Maria. Since coming to Puerto Natales, he had led a bachelor existence outside a couple of short, sharp liaisons with passing tourists.

Apart from licking his professional and personal wounds, Nacho was also glad to escape Santiago for a while. The urban sprawl, traffic, graffiti, and crowds had begun to get him down. He had recently gone up the Costanera Tower, the tallest building in South America, and from its viewing gallery he'd seen, and been appalled by, the visible brown haze of pollution that engulfed the city. At least here in Patagonia the strong winds ensured that no smog could develop. The windows rattled again as this thought crossed his mind.

Nacho quickly looked up a few things on the Internet using his laptop. He read his first search on Google and found out that Senator Towers was from the right wing of the Republican Party. He seemed to be anti-everything. Anti-abortion, anti-immigration, anti-environmental controls and was a climate-change denier and a keen supporter of President Trump. There were many pictures of the Senator at election rallies, white teeth gleaming in a rictus smile below a red baseball cap, a bouffant, well-dressed lady by his side.

He flipped to the CNN web page and read a short news article stating that Trump-surrogate Senator Dwayne Towers had been reported dead in "suspicious circumstances" in a Chilean national park by a journalist on the spot called Lev Zinczenko. The claim was said to be uncorroborated and there were no details as yet with communications to the site of death being problematic due to the remoteness of the location. A few talking heads had already expressed the usual "our thoughts and prayers are with the family at this difficult time" trite platitude.

A quick search for Lev Zinczenko revealed that he was a Ukrainian-born Pulitzer Prize-winning journalist who had recently been fired from the *Washington Recorder* newspaper after publishing a book entitled *Death of a Dream*, a supposed exposé of the decline of moral values inside the GOP. Nacho knew the GOP was short for "Grand Old Party", a self-aggrandising acronym of the American Republicans. It didn't sound like Zinczenko and Towers would have been on the same side politically.

He checked the Torres del Paine weather forecast. Wind, wind and more wind seemed to be the forecast's mantra. Gusts of over 120 kilometres per hour had been recorded earlier in the day. From his time living there, Nacho knew that gales up to 180 kilometres per hour were possible. He was not looking forward to the drive.

Finally, he visited the Último Hotel website as, although he had heard about it, it had been built since he was last in Torres del Paine. It billed itself as the ultimate hotel experience in the ultimate location, hence its name. Self-effacement didn't seem to be one of the Último's virtues. He put his laptop to sleep and closed the lid.

Nacho picked up a rucksack of clothes and personal gear which he kept on the offchance that he was sent on a case in the far reaches of the large province served by his unit. He'd packed it when he had first arrived at his new post and it was so far unused. He lifted a grab bag of what he called his "detective's tools of the trade" and added his laptop to its contents. He checked he had his wallet, police badge and smartphone, before putting on his outdoor jacket. Almost as an afterthought, Nacho opened his desk drawer and added his SIG P220 service pistol to his bag's contents. He hoped he wouldn't be needing it.

By the time he stepped out into the wind and rain, any thought of a nap and a quiet evening watching Netflix had evaporated, and his thoughts turned to his destination, Torres del Paine. Nacho had put off going up there in case its siren song sucked him into his old life, but now he had no excuse, and he felt excited to be going back to his spiritual home.

CHAPTER 2

Nacho edged his Defender out on to Carlos Bories and turned right along the one-way street. The Land Rover was army surplus and nearly ten years old, but it was reliable, and had only cost him twelve million pesos. It was exactly the right sort of vehicle for Patagonia with the region's mix of paved and dirt roads, variable weather, and limited infrastructure.

At the T-junction on the Canal Señoret waterfront, Nacho turned right again on to Pedro Montt for a few hundred metres, before stopping off to fill up the Defender's fuel tank with diesel. His next stop was at the Nomad Coffee Truck Stop, a converted motorhome, where he bought a large Americano and some muffins from Daniela. Enrique waved to him from the back of the little café, but Nacho had no time to talk to the friendly proprietors and headed out, now fully supplied for the three-hour journey to the park. He hoped the purchased caffeine and sugar fix would keep any leftover sleepiness from lunch at bay. Nacho circled the roundabout on the outskirts of Puerto Natales and took Route 9 north. He fumbled one-handedly with his smartphone until it connected to the rudimentary sound system he had self-installed in the Defender, and soon the opening bars of U2's "It's a Beautiful Day" filled the vehicle. As he looked at the weather, the irony of the song title made Nacho smile.

On his left, as he drove north, across the Seno de Última Esperanza, the Last Hope Sound, Nacho caught glimpses between the raindrops of the mountains of the Sierra Ballena, which were still snow-capped, even in the height of summer. The mountains represented the tail end of the Andes. He was soon passing the exit to Puerto Bories, where a brown information sign indicated the road to the remains of the Frigorifico factory. This old abattoir and mutton processing plant was a national monument to the days when sheep ruled the surrounding rolling landscape. Sheep had given way to cattle, and now vast ranches controlled the grazing on either side of the highway. The sheep farmers had driven off the native peoples and then been deposed themselves and, while Nacho appreciated the irony and liked a good steak, he wasn't sure that land ownership on such a grand scale was a good thing.

He drove carefully, mindful of what the DG had said about not involving any other forces of officialdom at this stage. The last thing he needed was for a Carabineros highway patrol to pick him up for speeding. He doubted, however, if many of his law enforcement colleagues would be out and about in their green and white patrol cars in weather like this.

The box-shaped Defender wasn't exactly aerodynamic, but the vehicle's tenacious four-wheel drive was a boon in the treacherous crosswinds which swept in from the west, off the Pacific Ocean. The winds made the steering wheel lively and Nacho had to keep a tight grip even if the road at this stage of his journey was straight for many long stretches. The windscreen wipers were set on their fastest speed, but visibility was poor, and he almost collided with a bus stop shelter which had been ripped off its foundations and blown onto the road. He caught a glimpse of its blue roof through a sweep of the wipers and just managed to stop in time without aquaplaning.

After twenty-five kilometres, he turned left on to the Y290 road. The main highway bent right towards the next town of Cerro Castillo, nearly fifty kilometres north-east on the Argentinian border, but Nacho's drive continued north.

A short while after the turn-off, he repeated his evasive action as a flock of rheas ran across the road in front of him, the large ostrich-like birds swerving like drunk men as they were buffeted by the wind and no doubt blinded by the rain. Nacho knew that somewhere to his right was Laguna Sofia, but it wasn't visible and he idly wondered if the lake's flamingoes could stand on one leg in such conditions. He suspected the pink birds were hunkered down in the reeds at the edge of the brackish lagoon with the ducks and other wildfowl.

As he drove on, Nacho's mind wandered to his past time in Torres del Paine. Before going to university he'd spent two years as a hiking guide at the Explora Hotel there. His memories of the stunning scenery of the national park were still fresh in his mind. The way the Paine Massif rose almost vertically from a foreground of turquoise lakes and beech forests was unlike any other view in the world. No wonder it was a UNESCO site. He knew the park was rated as the "Eighth Wonder of the World" by TripAdvisor and the "Fifth Best Sight in the World" by National Geographic. If it was the fifth, he couldn't imagine what the other four must be like. What fascinated Nacho was the constantly changing weather around the grandeur of the Paine Massif. The mountains were sometimes completely cloaked in misty clouds; at other times they stood out bold against an azure sky, with maybe the odd lenticular cloud hanging like a UFO above the peaks. Visitors often thought the guides were exaggerating when they said the park experienced all four seasons in one day, but they soon agreed after a few hours out on a hike. It wasn't uncommon to go from sunshine, to rain, to snow in a few hours, but always accompanied by strong winds.

At the Explora, Nacho had gone on a training course for several weeks after demonstrating his English language skills. He'd learned about geology, glaciology, the park's flora and fauna, the history of its exploration, the archeology of its original inhabitants, and all the different hiking routes, as well as first aid, and how to deal with difficult guests. While he didn't use these skills any more in his day job, they gave him a high appreciation of his natural surroundings wherever he travelled. His reverie was interrupted by a vehicle travelling in the opposite direction, which flashed its headlights at him as he approached. Nacho brought himself rapidly back into the present, finding he'd drifted over the road's median.

Unfortunately, the weather was so bad and visibility so poor that there was no point stopping at the mirador on Lago del Toro for a first view of the massif and so he drove on. Toro was the largest lake in the area and it straddled the park boundary. Out of his right-side window he could just see that its surface was being whipped up by the wind into a wild froth of white-capped breakers on top of a rolling swell, more reminiscent of the open sea. He proceeded into the park via the Serrano entrance and on to the Park Ranger Headquarters run by CONAF, the National Forest Corporation, some five kilometres further on.

The headquarters was a group of low-rise cream-coloured buildings with red roofs. Pick-up trucks and a shiny new fire engine, all with Park Ranger markings, were clustered in a parking lot beside what a sign identified as the administration building. Nacho couldn't see how one fire engine could stop the forest and bush fires that had occasionally devastated the park on a grand scale, but he mentally raised his hat to the brave souls who would make the attempt. Off to one side of the complex, a windsock stood beside a helipad, its orange sleeve stretched out horizontally, its canvas cracking in the wind, explaining why no investigators were flying in. He got out and ran through the pelting rain to the administration building.

'Well, well, look what the cat dragged in,' said the ranger behind the reception desk as Nacho entered.

'You're lucky I'm a pussycat and not a puma then,' replied Nacho. 'How have you been, Rafael? Long time no see.'

'It's been a few years. I heard you'd upped and joined the police after university, but I don't see no uniform.'

'That's because I'm PDI, not Carabineros, my friend. We're the brainy ones.'

'The brainy ones? Well, how did you get in then?' replied Rafael, laughing, before coming out from behind the desk. The two men hugged, back-slapped, and finally shook hands.

'It's good to see you, Nacho. We've missed you. The señoras have missed you too, I expect.'

'It's good to be back, even if it's not under the best of circumstances.'

'Ah, I get it. You've come about this Yankee politico?'

'Yeah, I'm up to see how he died. I'm to make sure it's okay for the body to be removed, so it can be repatriated.'

'Well, he's still up at Campamento Italiano, you know? The weather's been too bad to move him and none of the hotel catamarans have been running.'

'Shit. I'll have to get across somehow,' said Nacho. The Campamento Italiano was on the other side of Lago Pehoé from the Último Hotel. 'What about your boat? Will you try?'

'Maybe. It's a big ask, Nacho. You know this wind can flip a boat over if it gets under the hull. Let's see what the weather's like first thing tomorrow and I'll call you. It's forecast to be a bit better for a few hours in the morning before getting worse again. Where are you staying? Do you need a bunk here?'

'No, I'll be up at the Último. Thanks for the offer, though.'

'The Último? Very fancy.'

'I wouldn't mind some dinner though, if that's on offer.'

'Sure, come on, I'll race you across to the canteen.'

The two men braved the wind and rain and were soon ensconced in the canteen, enjoying a large plate of *curanto*, a stew of seafood, pork, and vegetables, livened up by Nacho's favourite aji chillies. They washed it down with mugs of coffee. Over dinner they reminisced about Nacho's time in the park, the big events there, like the fire of 2012, as well as some of the characters who worked in the park, and a few of the celebrity visitors. During the conversation, Rafael expressed his concern about the rising numbers of visitors and their impact.

'We're getting nearly a quarter of a million visitors every year now. Not all of them are what you might call "environmentally friendly". It's not just the risk of another big fire I'm worried about, it's the litter, especially the plastic that the animals are eating. Then there's the effect of all those hiking boots on the trails we're expected to maintain.'

'Yeah, I gather it's a problem all over the world. Too many tourists at all the favourite destinations. I was reading an article in *El Mercurio* the other day that Venice, over in Europe, may ban cruise ships, and that Barcelona was controlling numbers of visitors. I don't know what the solution is.'

After their last coffee, Nacho got up to leave. 'Look, Raphael, here's my card. It's got my mobile phone number on it.'

'Hmm, Inspector Hernández, eh? Aren't you a bit young for an inspector?'

'You know what they say, Rafael, "policemen look younger every day". I have to go. Call me about the boat. As early as you like. I'll be ready. I really need to get over there, my friend.'

Nacho got back into his Defender. It was getting late now, and although being so far south meant the sun set close to ten o'clock, it was dark enough for him to put on his headlights before continuing deeper into the park. He crossed the Puente Weber bridge and drove alongside the Rio Paine for a few kilometres before passing his old employer, the Explora Hotel. It was one of the first eco-hotels in the world, and Nacho was proud to have worked there. He left the low white building beside the Salto Chico waterfall behind him, and soon found himself driving into the parking lot of the Último Hotel. It was located on the site of an old campground. The poor had been displaced to make way for the rich. *Nothing new there*, thought Nacho.

From his Internet search before he had left Puerto Natales, Nacho felt he knew all about the hotel. Its architecture and interior design were apparently a fusion of Scandinavian and Chilean, using local woods, stones, and native textiles and ceramics. From what he could see on its website, its rack rate made sure it was very exclusive. Every room had a picture window with an electric blind controlled from the bed. A flick of the switch and the blind would lift at sunrise to reveal the best view in the world – the Cuernos del Paine with the turquoise of Lago Pehoé in front and backlit by the pink of clouds bathed in the early morning sunlight. All of this "visible without so much as leaving your bed" said the hotel's advertising blurb. When not admiring the view from bed, guests could luxuriate on their private balcony with its personal hot tub. The hotel had its own corps of guides to help with hikes and gauchos to help with horse riding. The bar and the only Michelin three-star restaurant in South America looked on to the same breathtaking view as the bedrooms. Its wine cellar of the finest Chilean vintages was to die for according to the resident sommelier's own rhetoric. The hotel's environmental credentials were enhanced by its fleet of electric vehicles, an electric catamaran, and solar panels built into the building's roof. Nacho admired the hotel's environmental credentials, but hated its pretentiousness. Even before he entered it, he'd decided that he wouldn't like it or the people who stayed there.

CHAPTER 3

Crossing the hotel threshold, Nacho was met by a concierge who blocked his way. The man obviously thought Nacho's jeans, trainers and old anorak were not befitting attire for one of his guests.

'Can I help you, sir?' the concierge asked in a condescending way, as if dealing with a lunatic who had wandered into the wrong building.

'I'm sure you can. Police. Inspector Hernández, PDI. I'd like to talk to your manager, please,' replied Nacho, holding out his silver badge emblazoned with the national coat of arms.

The man recoiled as if bitten by a snake, and Nacho wondered if the concierge was an ex-con, given the startled reaction. His own lapel badge identified the concierge as Andrés Bravo, and Nacho instinctively made a mental note of the name.

'I'll get Señor Gutiérrez for you right away, sir,' said the concierge, and he went behind a desk to make a short call on a house phone.

A few minutes later, a tall individual in his early forties with dark, slicked-back hair, a gliding gait, and a badge saying "Luis Hernan Gutiérrez, Manager" on it, arrived in front of Nacho. The man offered a damp handshake and an invitation to his office.

'As you will have gathered, I'm here about Senator Towers,' said Nacho once they were seated in the manager's office. 'Can you tell me what happened?'

'I don't know exactly what happened. The Senator was out on a hike. His guide called in to the hotel around lunchtime that a guest had died. He identified the deceased as Mr Towers, and that he didn't know how the Senator had died.'

'Well, I've been asked to investigate his alleged "suspicious death". Did the guide say anything to indicate why it may have been suspicious?'

'No, he didn't. That awful reporter, Mr Zinczenko, is responsible for that! I know a man in my position should not talk ill of his guests, but why he made that statement on Twitter I cannot imagine. Unfortunately, it was my sad duty to tell the Senator's wife. Mrs Towers was quite distraught when I told her, and several of her friends have been comforting her. I'm sure the journalist heard the news from one of them,' said Gutiérrez, shaking his head, a look of annoyance on his face.

'Then what did you do?'

'Well, I called the police of course, and got through to the PDI in Punta Arenas. They said that, given a US politician was involved, they would have to get in touch with Santiago. I presume that's why you're here? They eventually called me back to say an investigator would be sent up to us.'

'Correct, Santiago assigned me. Now, after calling us, what did you do?'

'Alas, I then had to tell the hiking party with the Senator to stay where they were as we couldn't get a boat across the lake to collect them. It was too dangerous. Our captain said there was a high risk of capsizing. The last thing I needed was more dead guests drowned in the lake in full view of the hotel. There's an old adage in the hotel trade, Inspector, that a dead guest is not a happy guest, and it's my job to keep the Último's guests very happy,' replied the manager, his lips twitching into a thin smile with the last sentence.

'After you heard about Zinczenko's tweet, what did you do?'

'Well, we've blocked all landline calls in and out of the hotel as other journalists and television reporters were trying to find out more. Guests can still contact their friends or media through their mobile phones or online, I'm sure, but they'll have nothing new to say. Unfortunately, it's already been on CNN, Fox News, BBC World, and our own TV Nacional and Canal 13. In the meantime, we've issued a blanket statement saying that we are waiting until the authorities investigate. That's where you come in, Inspector Hernández, as I expect you to placate the media.'

'So, you have no indication about what happened to the Senator?' asked Nacho, ignoring the manager's expectation and returning to the politician's death.

'I'm sure it was a heart attack. We ask all our guests to sign a waiver confirming their personal health so that we face no liability if something like this happens to them, particularly Americans. You know how litigious Americans are. They'll sue anybody at the drop of a hat. The Senator was in his seventies, after all. Thankfully, he wasn't officially part of the TripLux Party, so our relationship with the travel company should still hold good.'

'The TripLux Party?'

'Yes, TripLux. Have you never heard of them? They're a luxury tour company based in New York. They offer exclusive vacations to high-wealth individuals, flying between locations in their private jet, and staying at top-ranked hotels, like ours. We have a group here who are doing South America.'

'*Doing* South America? What do you mean?'

'I mean they're literally flying all over the continent to visit its most famous sites. They've done Tikal, Galapagos, Machu Pichu and the Atacama Desert, and now they're here. They're meant to be going the day after tomorrow to Buenos Aires, then on to the Iguazu Falls, before finishing in Rio. They've their own dedicated Boeing 737 sitting down at Puerto Arenas Airport. They're doing eight stops in twenty-four days. It's an amazing trip.'

Nacho thought it sounded like lunacy. No doubt the travellers could plaster their Facebook pages with selfies in front of some of the world's greatest cultural and natural landmarks and tell tales at cocktail and dinner parties about their exploits, but what would they learn about the countries they visited and how their people lived? He refocused on something Gutiérrez had said earlier.

'You just said that Senator Towers wasn't officially part of the TripLux party. What did you mean by that?'

'His wife is part of the TripLux group. The Senator was apparently on a fact-finding mission to Chile and opted to join his wife down here for a few days.'

'I see. And, as I understand it, from what you've indicated, and the rangers told me, the Senator's body is still over at the Campamento Italiano?'

'That's correct, along with the whole hiking party of seven other guests and one of our guides. They were doing the Valle del Francés trail. You have to take our catamaran from here across Lago Pehoé to the start and then get picked up by the same boat when you've finished. They went over early this morning. However, as I said earlier, the weather deteriorated and the wind's been too strong for our catamaran to cross and get them. None of the other boats was willing to risk it either.'

'Yes, I can understand that. It was a pretty grim drive up here.'

'It's been far worse today than was forecast. They'll have to spend the night there. How awful for them. It's hardly glamping! It doesn't really matter now, as we were told by your headquarters in Santiago to leave everything as it was over there until an officer got here and visited the scene of the crime. If indeed it was a crime. I still suspect it was a heart attack or a pre-existing condition, I really do.'

'Well, I'm hoping to go over there first thing tomorrow in the Rangers' boat. Now, can you tell me a bit more about the party that's over there.'

'I'll get Fernanda, our Head Guide, to brief you on that if you don't mind. I need to go and schmooze with my guests, particularly Mrs Towers. The poor woman is obviously very upset, and it's been made worse by the body not being brought back.'

'Please give her my condolences. I'll meet with her later on. Now, where do I meet this Fernanda?'

'Just go back to reception, and I'll ring her to meet you there.'

Nacho went back to the reception area and he was soon joined by a slim, raven-haired woman about his own age. Her golden skin seemed to glow, she flashed him a beautiful white smile, and Nacho felt his pulse quicken. She was wearing some sort of uniform of a khaki shirt which was badged with the hotel logo, green trekking pants, and sturdy hiking boots. She was carrying a tablet computer with her. As she approached, she held out her hand.

'Inspector Hernández, I'm Fernanda MacLeod, the Head Guide.'

'Pleased to meet you. Please, call me Nacho.'

They shook hands. Her grip was firm, and Nacho noted there were no rings on her fingers.

'OK, that's cool. And you can call me Señorita MacLeod.' She laughed at the expression on his face after she'd said this, and added, 'Just kidding. You can call me Fernanda, of course. Are you by any chance the Nacho Hernández who used to guide for the Explora?'

'Yes, I am,' said Nacho, surprised. 'I left a few years ago, went to university, and then joined the PDI.'

'Well, I was your replacement over there. I moved up here to the Último as Head Guide when it opened.'

'Small world,' said Nacho, who was having difficulty not staring into her dark eyes.

Fernanda led him to a large table which seemed to have a computer touch screen as its top. The screen was showing a map of the whole Torres del Paine National Park.

'I gather you're here about Senator Towers? Such a tragedy. It's never happened to me before. I've never lost a guest. All our guests self-declare themselves healthy. I saw Senator Towers, and I must admit I thought he looked a very fit man for his age. He and seven other guests went off early this morning to do the Valle del Francés.'

As she was speaking, Fernanda was using her fingertips to expand the map on the table screen to show only the hotel, Lago Pehoé, and the south-west corner of the Paine Massif. She was pointing to the valley between Cerro Paine Grande and the Cuernos del Paine.

'Who was in the party?' asked Nacho.

Fernanda looked at her tablet before speaking. 'Our guide, Hugo Sánchez, very experienced, very personable, a chemist turned zoologist by training, about our age, assuming you're about thirty. He had six Americans and two others in his party. The Americans were Senator Towers, plus Taylor Burroughs, Randy Thompson, Hester Wilson, Mo Ismail and Miranda Alexandra, the actor. All from the TripLux tour group.'

'Who were the other two?'

'One is an Australian called Jim Sullivan, and the other guy is an Englishman called Callum Henderson.'

'And they're still at the Campamento Italiano?'

'Yes, they'd stopped there in the beech forest behind the campsite to eat lunch and use the toilets before going on up the valley to see the glaciers on Paine Grande. They weren't going all the way up to the Campamento Británico,' said Fernanda, pointing at the map.

'And what does your guide say happened? I presume you're in radio contact? Mobile phone reception's not good over there, as I recall.'

'Yes, I was the person Hugo called first with the news. That's our protocol if a guest takes ill. He said the Senator went to the toilet in the middle of lunch and never came out. Hugo went to investigate and found the Senator dead inside the hut. He, and some of the guests, I presume, brought the body out and transferred it to the camp's registration hut and alerted the rangers there. It was after that, that Hugo radioed me with the sad news and I told our manager, Mr Gutiérrez. Unfortunately, the wind got up and no boat could get across to them, and then we got the message to tell them to stay there anyway, until the police arrived. And now you have.'

'Yes, well, I've arrived here, but not over there. If the wind dies down for a period, as expected tomorrow morning, I've commandeered the Rangers' boat to go over there. It's predicted to be still too bad for your catamaran, but I expect we'll give it a go. I'll have to look at the site and the corpse and take preliminary statements from the hiking party before we bring the body back.'

'I'll come with you if you like. I'd like to see how Hugo is. I'm his boss, after all.'

'Fine. Now where do I sleep? It's been a long drive and we may have an early start.'

'I'll show you to where we guides sleep. Mr Gutiérrez allocated a room over there in our accommodation block for you. We each have our own rooms and even an en suite shower room. Very luxurious. My next door neighbour is on rotation out of here and has gone home to Valparaiso. You can have his room.'

'Sounds good to me, thank you.'

CHAPTER 4

Early the next morning, Nacho received a call from Rafael telling him they could take the Rangers' boat over to the other side of the lake to the start of the Valle del Francés trail, but they would have to leave by 7am. The forecast was predicting a weather window of slightly lower winds until early afternoon. They could make the lake crossing, hike to the Campamento Italiano, spend an hour at the most there, come back, and be across the lake within the window, but it would be tight. Nacho elected to go for it, heartened slightly by the fact that the rain had stopped.

Nacho had enjoyed a good night's sleep, tired after his drive. He'd called the DG to confirm that he'd arrived in Torres del Paine, before putting the light out. His dreams had featured Fernanda, and he wondered if they should be reclassified as fantasies. As they enjoyed a quick breakfast together, Nacho was glad that Fernanda in the flesh was as attractive as in his reveries.

Just after seven o'clock, Nacho and Fernanda left the hotel's private dock on the Rangers' ten-metre catamaran with Rafael as crew and the boat's captain, Arturo, at the wheel. Normally, Nacho preferred to sit outside on small boats, being slightly claustrophobic and with a tendency to seasickness, but the wind was too fierce, and so he went down into the cabin with the others. The crossing was one of the roughest he had ever experienced. He was glad he was wearing a life vest for it felt like the catamaran might somersault at any time and they'd all end up in the chilly waters of Lago Pehoé. The boat thumped its way from wave crest to wave crest across the rough lake and one time fell so far and so fast that Nacho bumped his head on the cabin roof, much to the amusement of his colleagues. After twenty hull-slamming minutes, they finally reached the pier at the Lodge de Montaña Paine Grande on the other side of the lake.

Nacho, Fernanda and Rafael disembarked, leaving Arturo to look after the boat. They had a quick toilet stop at the refuge. There were only a few hearty souls around the large building of bleached wood and glass, and fewer still crawling around its adjacent campsite, checking that their low yellow tents were pegged down to survive the ferocious wind.

Before setting off again, Nacho and his companions put on extra layers, re-hitched their rucksacks, and adjusted their walking poles, necessary accessories for extra stability in the wind. They set off on a marked hiking trail parallel to the lake shore before climbing upwards across a headland. The trees around them were all silver-grey, relics of the devastating fire of 2012. On the skyline the twisted wooden trunks and branches created weird and eerie silhouettes against the white clouds scudding overhead. The standing trees were all bent in the same direction, compasses pointing to the east under the prevailing westerly wind. Many of the fallen trees were cloaked in Barba de Viejo, the dead wood providing a perfect substrate for the creeping mats of wispy moss. Although the forest of lenga and ñirre had not recovered in the intervening eight years, the lower vegetation of bushes and shrubs was flourishing, and there was even the odd dash of colour from the red flowers of the firetree. Below the bushes, the ground was covered in coarse grass illuminated by the bright yellow of dandelions which seemed to grow everywhere. Occasionally, the party paused briefly to refresh themselves on bilberries from the low-lying calafate bushes and to sip from their water flasks. Since they were heading east, the climb was wind-assisted, and they made good time.

After their short ascent, they reached a mirador and Lago Scöttsberg, named for the Swedish cartographer who had first mapped it, lay in front of them. Beyond it, were the Cuernos del Paine, the famous Horns of the main Paine Massif. As if by a miracle, the cloud lifted and the Horns could be seen in all their glory. The mountains had been sculpted by nature into a compact block with multiple spires, several reaching to over 2,000 metres. The caps of the mountains were black due to remnants of a rock that Nacho had learned to call hornfels. The main walls of the massif were pink granite, sheer in many locations, but carved into u-shaped valleys by glaciers in other places. The base of the mountains was a grey granodiorite, if Nacho remembered his geology lessons correctly. Even though Nacho had seen this sight hundreds of times, it was still breathtaking. Alas, the famous towers that had given the park its name couldn't be seen and were on the other side of the massif. Then, as if by sleight of hand, the mountains disappeared once more into cloud.

The next stage of their hike took them closer to the lake. The waters were being whipped up into a fine spray and small whirlpools of water sprites danced across the surface. By now they were out of the fire-affected zone and walking through a fresh green mountain beech forest. As before, every tree was bent in the same direction, evidence of the perpetual wind.

After skirting the lake, they arrived, less than two hours after disembarking, at a suspension bridge. The bridge crossed the Rio del Francés, which was a raging torrent below, its glacial meltwaters swollen by the recent rain. The bridge had seen better days and was only strong enough for one person to cross at a time. The wire cables holding the bridge in situ were frayed in places and the walkway looked like it had been laid by a drunken carpenter using shipwrecked driftwood. Nacho commented on the bridge's poor state, and Rafael defended his rangers by stating that budgets were tight and that CONAF was underfunded. They crossed one by one, the bridge swaying and bucking beneath their feet, the walkway slippery by spray from the cascade below.

On the other side, they quickly reached the Campamento Italiano, a collection of huts in a deserted campsite. The camp got its name from its history as the base for Italian mountaineers. The Italians had been in competition with their British peers to conquer the famous Torres del Paine and the other peaks of the massif in the middle of the previous century.

Rafael led them to the registration building and they entered a large hut. Inside, they found two rangers and eight sorry-looking individuals plus a shape under a silver foil survival blanket, and which Nacho took to be the late Senator Towers. The faces all looked up expectantly at Nacho and his companions. Nacho addressed them in English.

'Good morning, everyone. I am Inspector Hernández of the Chilean Investigations Police. This is Rafael Vidal, the head of the Park Rangers, and I believe you know Fernanda MacLeod, from your hotel.'

Everyone started to speak at once and Nacho had to shout in English for calm. 'Look, I understand you all want to get out of here as soon as possible. You have my condolences, and I recognise you've all had a traumatic time and a very uncomfortable night. Before we leave though, I have a few questions, and I'll need to look at Senator Tower's body. In the meantime, while I do that, Fernanda here has some hot food sent up by the hotel, as well as chocolate and snacks so you can eat and refresh yourselves before we hike to the boat. We need you energized because we only have a short period to get back to the lodge and across the lake before the weather closes in again, and so we'll need to walk at a fairly rapid pace.'

Fernanda set up shop at the registration desk and handed out insulated canisters containing hot chicken and rice and poured out piping hot lentil soup from a flask.

Nacho had Rafael help him carry the Senator's corpse outside and they removed the blanket after putting on latex gloves Nacho had brought. The Senator was fully dressed in the best quality outdoor gear and someone had hitched up his trousers after he'd been found

27

in a half-clothed state. The man's face was contorted as if in great pain and his fists were clenched. Rigor mortis had set in and the body was difficult to deal with, but, after inspection, Nacho could see no wounds on the body and no evidence of trauma to the head. It certainly didn't look like he had been shot or stabbed. He took several pictures of the corpse with his phone, before calling for Hugo, the guide who had found the Senator.

'Hello, Hugo. Look, I know this must be very distressing for you. No guide likes to lose a guest. I used to be a guide here in the park myself and so I know how you must feel. However, I have a few questions for you. Do you feel up to answering them?'

Hugo nodded.

'Can you tell me what happened?' Nacho asked.

'Well, we had stopped for lunch. Usually, on this walk, we stop out on the moraine after the forest so guests can eat and soak in the view of the glaciers to their left and the Horns to their right. Yesterday it was too windy, and so I decided we'd stop and eat in the forest. We sat up there, upwind of the toilets of course,' replied Hugo. He pointed as he spoke to a collection of small grey wooden huts which housed the camp's chemical toilets. The guide had an unusual accent that Nacho couldn't place, and he thought Hugo must be from up north, near the border with Peru or Bolivia.

'I set out a blanket and invited everyone to get out their canister of hot food and I distributed cutlery. I offered them tomato soup from my flask and passed round bread and chilli-salt. Then we all began to eat. At some point the Senator got up saying he wasn't feeling well and headed off to one of the toilets. He was away for some time, and I got worried. I went to the hut and knocked on the door. There was no reply. I used my knife to undo the lock and opened the door. He was slumped against the side of the hut. He didn't answer me when I asked if he was all right. I touched him, and he didn't react, so I felt for the pulse in his neck and there wasn't one. I went back to the guests and told them I thought the Senator was dead. They were all shocked. I think one or two of the women might have started crying.

Mr Henderson accompanied me back to the toilet and confirmed the Senator was dead. Henderson lifted the Senator off the seat and I pulled up his boxers and trousers. We then carried him to the hut and covered him with my emergency blanket.'

Hugo stopped. He was staring into space, and Nacho wondered if he was in shock. 'And then what happened?' Nacho asked, nudging the guide forward with his story.

'Then I got on the radio and called the hotel. There's no mobile signal over here in the valley. The hotel said to wait until they checked a few things. They expected that I would have to bring the guests back and leave the body here. However, they then came back and told me the boat couldn't make it because of the wind, and that we were to wait here for further instructions. They came on again later and said someone had claimed the death was "suspicious" and that I was to wait here with the guests and body. I was told I wasn't to risk taking them to the refuge in the bad weather as we couldn't afford to lose another guest. They also said the police had been informed and that they would arrive tomorrow, that is today, weather permitting.'

'And do you know who was sitting beside the Senator at the lunch?'

'Yes, I actually have a picture. I took a photo on my phone,' replied Hugo and he pulled out his smartphone and showed Nacho a photograph. Nacho took the phone for a better look.

In the picture, the party of eight guests was arrayed in a semicircle facing the photographer. On the right there were three women sitting together, one young, one quite old and one of indeterminate age. Senator Towers was easy to spot. He was laughing, and seemed at ease with a group, like most politicians. He was on the far left with a small weather-beaten male by his side, and two other males slightly behind him.

'Who are these guests around the Senator?' asked Nacho.

'On his left is Mr Sullivan. He's an Australian. He's a regular visitor here. Behind the Senator on the right is Mr Thompson. He's with the American tour group. The other man behind the Senator is Mr Henderson. He's English.'

'And who is this?' asked Nacho pointing at the only black face in the group. The man was staring at the Senator, a look of unabashed hatred on his face.

'That's Mr Ismail. He and the Senator had a row on the way up here.'

'What about?'

'I can't tell you. I was at the front, leading, and I could hear them shouting at each other behind me. It must have been quite heated because I heard them over the wind, but it wasn't distinct enough for me to know what it was about.'

'Do you mind if I send a copy of this to myself?' asked Nacho, and he forwarded it anyway, before Hugo replied in the affirmative.

Since Nacho had seen no evidence of any wounds, he concluded that the Senator had either died of natural causes, or had been strangled or poisoned, so he asked Hugo some related questions.

'Did anyone else go to the toilet when the Senator was in his closet?'

'Yes, I think Mr Thompson and Mr Ismail went.'

'Wait here, please, Hugo,' instructed Nacho.

Nacho went back to look at the Senator's corpse. He pulled down the scarf at the neck and could see some evidence of contusion there. He took another photograph. He wondered if the American had been strangled. Next, he went to the wooden hut that Hugo had indicated was the scene of the Senator's demise. He opened the door and the stench hit him. He looked around inside quickly. It was like any other remote toilet, with a wooden seat perched above a pit of urine, excrement, and strong chemicals emitting an unforgettable miasma. No blood splatter or dried red stains anywhere supported the lack of visible wounds. There was a hole in the planking at the back of the hut. Nacho guesstimated that it would be at neck height for a sitting, or should that be shitting, Towers. He smiled briefly at his own joke. *Could someone have got a hand or hands in there to strangle the politician?* he wondered. Possibly. He took a photograph of the hole, holding a penknife beside it for scale. *If not strangulation, then poisoning?* he asked himself. He went back to where Hugo was waiting.

'Where are the canisters the food for your picnic came in?' Nacho asked the guide.

'They're inside. We washed them out in the river after finishing them last night.'

'Including the Senator's?' asked Nacho, his anger rising as he realised any evidence of poisoning may have disappeared. 'Damn it, that may have been critical evidence you've destroyed, you idiot.'

Hugo looked alarmed and stammered, 'I'm sorry, it's what we always do on hikes. I wasn't thinking. We all assumed he'd had a heart attack. Are you saying he didn't?'

'I'm saying that I don't know, but I would have liked to have all the evidence to make an informed decision and to have had what the Senator ate tested in a lab.' Nacho calmed down and spoke to Hugo again. 'Right, let's get going. I'll talk to the other guests once we get back to the hotel. We haven't got time for me to interview them all here. We need to get them and the body back to the boat so we can cross the lake before the weather closes in again.'

'Thank goodness for that. The guests will be relieved. One or two of them were muttering last night about the body being in the same room as them. I explained we couldn't leave it outside in case any pumas or foxes came by. That only alarmed them even more, and I had to escort each female guest to and from the toilets.'

Inside the hut, the hiking party seemed a little cheerier after their sustenance. Rafael had found the camp's first aid stretcher and he and Nacho laid the Senator out on it and tied the survival blanket around him. Rafael had decided to close the camp and proposed two pairs of stretcher bearers, one team being the two campsite rangers, and the other being Nacho and himself. Hugo also volunteered along with Henderson to help spread the effort further.

'You really don't mind?' Nacho asked the Englishman.

'Not at all. I've seen quite a few dead bodies in my time and done a fair bit of yomping with wounded on my back,' replied Henderson.

'Yomping?'

'British military slang for walking across the bush.'

Fernanda led the other guests off on their hike to the boat pier. It was going to be a difficult journey into the wind for much of the way. After a five-minute gap, Nacho and the other stretcher bearers set off with the body. The first obstacle faced was the suspension bridge. The camp rangers offered to carry the loaded stretcher over the swinging structure as they were the most used to crossing it. If it hadn't been such a serious business, Nacho thought their traverse would have make a good slapstick comedy routine as they staggered across like two drunks. They danced two steps forward and then one step back, precariously carrying their awkward load and almost dropping the body into the river on more than one occasion. All the time the bridge was swinging like a pendulum, and some strands of the supporting cables sprung apart with a loud "ping". Eventually, the rangers successfully made it to the other side with their load intact, much to Nacho's relief. After two and a half hours, swapping pairs every twenty minutes, they covered the eight kilometres to the catamaran. It was a tough slog into the teeth of the gale, and all the bearers were exhausted by the time they got back to the pier, where they reunited with Fernanda and her hiking party. The Rangers' boat had its powerful diesels running as it waited, and as soon as everyone was aboard, Arturo opened the throttles and the catamaran set off.

The whole group then had a thirty-minute rollercoaster ride across Lago Pehoé, back to the hotel's dock. A couple of the guests threw up on the way, which didn't make the crossing any easier for the others to bear in the enclosed cabin. It was late afternoon by the time everyone was back onshore, some greener than others. Waiting hotel staff were on-hand to whisk the distressed guests away, but before they did so, Nacho warned them all that he would have to interview them later that evening.

CHAPTER 5

After getting the body off the catamaran, Nacho asked the rangers to take the Senator up to the rear door of the hotel. The manager, Gutiérrez, met them there and led them to a meeting room in the hotel's conference suite where the body was laid out on the table. The silver survival blanket was replaced by a white sheet. Nacho had the hotel manager fetch the newly-widowed Mrs Towers, and the lady was ushered into the room.

The widow, when she arrived, looked like she was in her fifties, but was probably in her late sixties, thought Nacho, as he knew that many rich American ladies had plastic surgery and Botox injections. Her husband had been in his early seventies, and so unless she was a child bride, he thought his estimate was probably correct. She was heavily made up over a slightly orange, possibly sun-lamp derived, tan, and her blonde hair was almost certainly dyed. Her clothes and poise gave her a certain elegance. Nacho could see that she would make a good-looking partner for a politician anxious for well-staged, vote-winning photo opportunities. At least Towers hadn't traded her in for a younger model like so many of his ilk. *At least not overtly*, thought Nacho.

'Hello, Mrs Towers. I am Inspector Hernández of the Chilean Investigations Police. On behalf of myself and my government, may

I express our deepest condolences,' offered Nacho as she came to the head of the table.

She turned to look away from the shrouded figure and up at Nacho. He was surprised to see no red-rimmed eyes, no tears, and no obvious grief. 'Thank you. Now let's get this over with, shall we?' she said tersely.

'Of course, Señora. I realise this is a formality, but I have to ask you to confirm that this is indeed the body of your husband, Senator Dwayne Towers.' With that, Nacho raised a corner of the sheet to reveal the Senator's face.

'Jeez, he looks like he's seen a ghost. Poor old Dwayne. Yes, that's him.'

'Thank you, Señora. That will be all for now. I may have some questions for you later.'

'Do you think he was murdered? What's all this about "suspicious circumstances"? I thought he'd been found in some camp john. I thought he'd had a heart attack or something.'

'We're not sure yet, Señora. It may have been a heart attack or some other illness, or it may indeed be suspicious, I'm sorry to say. We just don't know yet.'

'Dwayne was as strong as an ox. He'd had a medical just recently. Was crowing about it to all and sundry. Maybe it was murder, for I doubt it was natural causes knowing the man.'

'It's very interesting you should say that, Señora. I'll bear it in mind. Thank you for your time right now, Mrs Towers, and, again, my condolences on your loss.'

As Mrs Towers left, Rafael stepped into the room, a grim look on his face.

'Bad news, I'm afraid, Nacho. The bridge on 290 is blocked. You know the one just south of Estancia Complejo?'

'Sure. What happened?'

'A cattle road train going south got caught in a strong gust while on the bridge and tipped over. Apparently, it's mayhem. The driver's severely injured and on his way back to the hospital in Puerto Natales, but there are dead and injured cattle all over the place and a good many have probably drowned in the river. The tractor unit smashed the safety barrier and is jammed in tight and the trailers are jackknifed across the road. It'll need a heavy crane to lift it all out of the way, and that will be impossible until the winds die down. To make matters worse, there's been a landslip on the other road into the park from Cerro Castillo, so we're isolated here for a couple of days I'd guess.'

'What about helicopters?'

'No way. The crosswinds are too severe,' said Rafael, shaking his head.

'Right, I suppose I'd better continue my investigations. At least the US Cavalry won't be arriving any time soon.'

'The US Cavalry? You've been watching too many movies, my friend.'

'Just a turn of phrase, Rafael,' lied Nacho. 'Thanks for the information.'

Inwardly, Nacho cursed the DG for not letting him bring a forensics team with him to the hotel, but then he had an idea. He went in search of the hotel manager once more.

'Señor Gutiérrez, do you know if you have a doctor within your guests, by any chance?' asked Nacho, after locating the manager in his office.

'I'm not sure, I'll have a look,' replied Gutiérrez, and he consulted his computer screen. 'Yes, it appears we do. Dr Alwyn Ifor Morgan. British passport. He's in room 22. I'll take you to him.'

The manager led Nacho out to reception and passed the bar area. A man was sitting at one of the picture windows with binoculars at his eyes surveying the massif, which had made a reappearance through the clouds.

'Ah, there's Dr Morgan,' said the manager, pointing at the guest with binoculars. He switched to English. 'Dr Morgan? Sorry to disturb your bird watching, but this gentleman would like a word with you.'

The man turned around, a look of surprise on his face and said,

'Bird watching? Me? No, I'm no twitcher, I was just looking at the mountains. How can I help?' asked Morgan, and he stood up and shook hands with Nacho.

'I'll leave you two to it,' said Gutiérrez and departed.

'Hello, Dr Morgan, my name is Hernández, and I'm a police inspector,' said Nacho holding up his badge.

The doctor went white and swayed, before asking, 'Oh, my goodness, have we done something wrong? Has something happened at home? Are my daughters okay? What is it?'

'No, it's okay, Dr Morgan, it's just that I need your assistance. I'm afraid there's been a death and I would like you to view the body and give me your professional opinion on how the person may have died.'

'Ah, thank God. I was worried there,' said Morgan, and then he laughed. 'I'm sorry, but I can't help you there.'

'But you are *Doctor* Morgan, right?'

'I am indeed, as in Dr Alwyn Morgan, PhD, sedimentology lecturer at the University of Reading, brackets, retired.'

'Ah, right, sorry,' said Nacho, and he could hardly hide his disappointment.

'Yes, we've just come off a Hurtigruten Antarctic cruise. I used to work down there in my early career with the British Antarctic Survey, but the wife had never been. Then I persuaded her to come here after our voyage. Fascinating place. It was on my bucket list.'

'Bucket list?'

'Yes, you know, your list of things you want to do or see before you "kick the bucket". Your "bucket list".'

Nacho surmised that "kick the bucket" must be an English euphemism for dying, but it wasn't a phrase he was familiar with. Meanwhile Morgan was continuing.

'You see, I'm an expert in the effect of plutonic rocks on sediments. What we geologists call the metamorphic aureole, and you have some great examples here.'

'Like the hornfels on the top of the Horns?'

'Yes, exactly!' exclaimed Morgan, surprised by Nacho's

knowledge. 'You said you were a policeman. Are you an amateur geologist too?'

'No, I'm afraid I've just displayed my total knowledge of metamorphic rocks gained from when I was a guide here in the park before university,' explained Nacho. 'I'll leave you to your observations. Sorry for disturbing you, Dr Morgan.'

As Nacho turned way, Morgan spoke again. 'But the wife could maybe help you.'

'Your wife?' asked Nacho, turning back to face the doctor.

'Yes, she's a retired doctor too, only a medical one, a former GP.'

Nacho cursed the manager's registration system for its male bias.

'Ah, here she comes now. Bethan, this man here needs your help. He's police and he needs a medical opinion, and I guess you're it around here. What did you say your name was, young man?'

'Hello, Dr Morgan, I'm Inspector Hernández,' said Nacho, holding out his hand to a plump lady with short grey hair. She was dressed in outdoor gear with her only fashion accessory being her bright red spectacles on a gold chain around her neck.

'How can I help?' asked the newcomer. This Dr Morgan seemed brisk and to the point where her husband, the other Dr Morgan, seemed loquacious.

'I'm afraid one of the hotel guests has died.'

'Ah, yes. I heard a rumour about that from the waitress at breakfast this morning.'

'I need an opinion on how it may have happened, and whether it was due to natural causes. I realise this is an imposition on you, Doctor, but I'm afraid the main road out of here to a pathologist is blocked, and the weather is making all travel difficult, even for a local medic to come here from Cerro Castillo, the nearby border town.'

'Yes, of course. I must warn you that I'm a GP, a general practitioner, not a specialist in this sort of thing. However, over my forty-year career I've had to sign quite a few death certificates, including for one or two murder victims, so I'll give it a go.'

'Thank you, please follow me.'

'You all right there, Alwyn? I'm just popping off to look at a cadaver with this young man,' the doctor said to her husband.

'Yes, yes, dear, go ahead,' said her spouse, engrossed in the mountains while waving his hand vaguely in the direction of his wife. 'I'm just doing a bit of Swiss geology and studying the contact on top of the Horns while it's not covered in clouds.'

Nacho led Dr Morgan to the meeting room where Senator Towers was lying and they made small talk along the way.

'Your English is very good, Inspector, if you don't mind me saying so. You sound quite British. Most English speakers we've met in South America speak with American accents.'

'My mother was an English teacher. She insisted I learn what she called "The Queen's English". She thought it was the proper version of the language. As a result, we watched British TV programmes where possible, saw British films at the cinema and ignored the subtitles, and listened to the BBC World Service. She hated British films dubbed into Spanish and insisted on finding what she called "unadulterated versions" in art cinemas in Santiago.'

'Well, it worked, and you sound quite posh.'

'Thank you, Doctor,' said Nacho, wondering if this was a compliment, as he knew that for some English people being posh was a bit of an insult.

They arrived at the temporary morgue and, before they entered, Nacho said, 'Due to the sensitivity around the person we're about to examine, I must ask you, Doctor, to please keep this confidential.'

'Yes, of course. Not a problem. Patient-doctor confidentiality, even for the dead ones, eh?'

They went in and Nacho removed the sheet covering Senator Towers. He pulled out two pairs of latex gloves and they put them on.

'And who exactly is this fellow?' asked Dr Morgan as she started to look at the body.

'He's a US senator by the name of Dwayne Towers. He's quite a famous politician in America.'

'A senator! Well, I've never heard of him. I have enough trouble keeping up with politics in Britain, what with Boris, Brexit and all.'

'We know he died at lunchtime yesterday, around noon.'

'Well, well, the poor chap looks like that fellow in *The Scream.*'

'You mean that famous painting?'

'Yes, the one by Munch. Alwyn and I saw the original last year in Oslo. Very small it was. Now let's see. Help me turn him over. You said he died about noon, yesterday? Well, that explains the rigor mortis. I can't see any obvious wounds and there are no blows to the head. Do we know what he was doing when he died?'

'He was sitting on the toilet.'

'Ah, "died at stool", as they say. Quite a few elderly people die while straining on the loo, but this chap looks quite healthy, actually, apart from being dead and having a face like he's seen the Devil. American, did you say? Well, he's not obese like so many of his countrymen. I'd guess he's a fit late-sixties.'

'Yes, that's about right, he's actually early seventies.'

'His hands are clenched tight too. I'd say he was in considerable pain when he died. Towers of Pain, eh!'

'It's Pie-Nay. Torres del Pie-Nay,' said Nacho, sounding slightly irritated. '"Pie-Nay" means "blue" in the language of the Tehuelche. Like the lakes here. The Tehuelche were the original inhabitants of this region.' Nacho stopped his lecture as he saw the slight smile on the doctor's lips and the twinkle in her eyes.

'Sorry, dear, just my little joke. I learned all about the Tehuelche from one of the guides on our walk yesterday,' she told him.

Nacho realised he had been exposed to the famous British sense of humour, and had shown that he maybe wasn't as clued up on idiomatic English language as he thought he was. His mother had warned him of the British love of irony, sarcasm, puns, and double meanings. It seemed like he had fallen for it this time.

'In some ways it looks like a heart attack, but I can't say for sure. He'd have to be opened up for a full autopsy. Do you have a torch, dear? I want to look down his throat to see if he choked on anything.'

39

'Not as such, but there's one on my phone.' Nacho pressed the torch symbol on his smartphone and the bright light at the back came on. He handed it to the doctor, who took it and shone the light inside the Senator's mouth.

'Hmm, there's some signs of burning inside his mouth. How could that be? Maybe he's taken some sort of corrosive chemical by mistake or poison. He was found on the loo, you say? Was there bleach or something in there? Doesn't smell like bleach though, as you'd expect some residual aroma coming up from his stomach. Also, it's usually kids who swallow bleach by mistake. But, then again, I've never seen a corpse where the mouth has been locked open like this. Usually we're trying to prise the lips and teeth apart to see inside a dead person's mouth.'

'What about those marks on his neck?'

'Ah, well spotted, young man. Yes, there's some contusion of the neck. Maybe he was strangled? But then his clenched fists are unusual as you'd have expected him to have been clawing at an assailant, wouldn't you? A full autopsy could tell from the scrapings they take under the fingernails if there's another person's skin under them. My best guess, based on a cursory look, is that your man here was most likely poisoned, but may have been strangled. He certainly wasn't shot, stabbed, or coshed. It could have been a heart attack or a ruptured brain aneurysm, but those mouth burns and the markings on his neck suggest otherwise. That's unless the shock of whatever burnt his mouth caused heart failure. I'm sorry I can't be more precise. You'll need a pathologist if you want more.'

'Thank you, Doctor. And again, please keep this examination confidential.'

'Of course. Mum's the word,' replied the doctor, confusing Nacho even more by introducing someone's mother into the conversation.

'Now, one more piece of advice. What do I do with him?' asked Nacho. 'The roads out of the park are blocked and won't be reopened for a day or two. I need to keep him fresh for a full autopsy.'

'You'll just have to bung him in the fridge, dear, like any other dead meat. You know, wrap him in clingfilm, stick him in a box, and put him in the cold store. A hotel this size must have a cold store.'

'Thank you, Doctor, you've been most helpful.'

Nacho followed Dr Morgan's suggestion, and had the kitchen deliver its widest roll of clingfilm. With Rafael's help, he wrapped the Senator up like a giant joint of beef. Next, he got the hotel's maintenance crew to make a temporary coffin from timber leftovers from the building's construction, and they placed the Senator in it. Finally, the Senator was put in the kitchen's walk-in cold store. Everyone involved was sworn to secrecy by the manager. The last thing Gutiérrez wanted was for his guests to think their prized Argentinian steak was coming from the same place as a corpse.

As Nacho came out of the kitchen and up through the restaurant, he was accosted by a tall figure who looked like the model for the KFC's Colonel Saunders. The man was dressed in jeans and a plaid shirt with a bootlace tie at his neck, a Stetson on his head, and cowboy boots on his feet. When he spoke, the man had a southern drawl to match his get-up.

'You that there detective?' asked the man, making it sound like Nacho was a "dee-tective".

'Yes, I'm Nacho Hernández. Can I help you, Señor?'

'Nacho? Like the corn chip?'

'Yes, but here in Chile it's a diminutive of Ignatius.'

'You talk like a Limey, son.'

'I can assure you I am Chilean, but I'm not your son. So, again, Señor, can I help you? I'm rather busy at the moment,' said Nacho, and he hoped his terse reply would get through to the man.

'And you're busy with what I want to talk to you about, son. I'm Howie Dawson, one of Dwayne Towers' oldest friends, and I want to tell you what I think happened to him.'

'In that case, why don't we sit at this table here?' suggested Nacho, intrigued, but sceptical that the man would have anything of value to add.

'Dwayne Towers was a good man. I've known him since we were Aggies together at Texas A&M,' said Dawson, fingering a large ring on

41

his finger as he spoke. Nacho recognised it as one of the graduation rings favoured by American college attendees. 'We were in the same frat house together. Went to 'Nam together, though he was a flyboy and I was PBI. Then he went into politics; followed his daddy. And I followed mine too, and went into the oil business. I helped Dwayne with the odd donation to be sure he got re-elected year after year. He was a solid supporter of the oil companies. Didn't stand for any of this green shit. Windmills and solar panels? How're they gonna power a decent-sized pick-up, eh? I feel so guilty now about what's happened to him.'

'Guilty? Why do you feel guilty, Mr Dawson?'

'Because I'm the one who persuaded him to join us down here. My wife and Miriam are the best of friends, you see.'

'Who's Miriam?'

'Why, Dwayne's wife, of course.'

'Ah, I'm sorry. I've met the poor lady, but didn't know her first name. Please, continue.'

'My wife, Stephanie, persuaded Miriam, and then me, to come. Told me TripLux were the world's best, and then I persuaded Dwayne to drop by. He was down here anyway on a fact-finding junket. Something to do with selling you guys more F-16 fighter jets. Usually he hates national parks. Thinks they stop exploitation of the Earth's natural resources as God intended. But, nevertheless, this time he came. We planned to go on the hike yesterday together, but my ulcer was playing up, and so I dropped out. He decided to go ahead. Biggest mistake he ever made. I'm telling you, son, Dwayne was set to succeed Trump in 2024.'

'Thank you, Mr Dawson, that's all very interesting, but you said you were going to tell me what happened to him.'

'Well, it was those eco-warriors, wasn't it? There's some of them on this trip and I'm sure they'll be some in this park. People like that has-been Miranda Alexandra. Or it could have been a damned immigrant like that Ismail guy. Damned foreigner from one of those shithole countries Trump was on about. He's exactly why we need a wall.'

'Mr Dawson, I must warn you that you can't use language like that here in Chile.'

'Or that faggot. Randy Thompson,' continued Dawson. 'Man dresses up like a woman for a living. What sort of person does that? A deviant does that!'

Nacho couldn't stand listening to this old, racist bigot any longer and got up to leave.

'I'm telling you it was one of those crazies, son. Dwayne was as fit as a fiddle. I don't often agree with that journalist, Zinczenko. The man's a goddamned communist! But this time I think he's right. Something suspicious has happened here. Dwayne was built like a brick shithouse.'

'That's a rather unfortunate analogy, Mr Dawson, given where he was found.'

'He'd just had a medical and was bragging about it at Mar-a-Lago only a few weeks ago. He even told me his sperm count was as high as it's ever been,' said Dawson, with a chuckle. 'You know he was the GOP's "Great White Hope" to succeed Trump, don't you? And I do mean "white", if you get my drift. You'd better find out who did this, Detective Corn Chip, or Washington will make sure you're crushed.'

Before Dawson had finished speaking, Nacho was off to the reception desk to find out where he could find Lev Zinczenko, the journalist. He found him in room 20.

CHAPTER 6

After knocking on the door and explaining who he was, Nacho was invited in. Zinczenko's room looked like a teenager's and the man himself reflected that untidiness in terms of rumpled dress, with his beer belly flopping over his straining waistband and his jeans stretched tightly across his thick thighs. He had unkempt grey hair, a wild beard, and dirty spectacles, and, unlike most Americans Nacho had met who had pristine smiles, his yellow teeth resembled old piano keys.

'So, you're investigating what happened to dear old Senator Towers, eh, Inspector Hernández?'

'Yes, Señor, and that's an investigation you triggered by your tweet about his death being "suspicious". Why did you write that?'

'Because the man had himself tweeted the results of his recent annual medical to the world, boasting about how fit he was, including that his cardiogram and other tests had shown him to have the heart of a thirty-year-old. Now, if that's true, then his death is suspicious, as that hike, although arduous for an overweight clinically-obese person like me, is not something that should have tested a fit thirty-year-old. On the other hand, if he was lying about his health – and he wouldn't be the first American politician to write his own medical report, let's face it – then a lie would be exposed. My job is to reveal lies, Inspector Hernández. It's what I do for a living.'

'And you're rather good at it, I believe. I read that you'd won the Pulitzer Prize a few years ago.'

'That was a slimmer cub reporter who won that. I outed various CIA-backed plans for regime change here in Latin America. This continent was my beat for many years. The Falklands War, the Argentinian juntas, Shining Path in Peru, Allende and Pinochet here in Chile – I covered them all.'

'That's quite a turbulent piece of our history you've witnessed, Señor.'

'History? Seems like only yesterday to me, but then I guess you're a lot younger.'

'And then what happened to you?' asked Nacho.

'Then I went back to DC. There, I was an ace reporter for the *Washington Recorder*, competing with the *Post* and the *New York Times* for the big political scoops. There's an old Chinese saying that the fish rots from the head down. Well, Capitol Hill can smell like a fish market these days. And then, a few months ago, I got fired after writing *Death of a Dream,* which outed the GOP instead of the CIA. The party's become a moral vacuum. However, I'm still not sure if it was the book, or the use of my family's Ukrainian connections to help lift the lid on Trump's shenanigans in my parents' home country.'

'And what do you do now?'

'Now? Now I'm a reluctantly retired journalist, blowing his final pay cheque on visiting Torres el Paine, one of the places I never got to, despite all my time in South America. And while I'm here, who should walk in the door but Dwayne Towers, who rapidly became the "late" Dwayne Towers. Now I have a scoop, the man-on-the-spot before the cable news guys get here, and maybe a way back to a job in DC. Who knows where this one will lead?'

'And what was Senator Towers really like? I've read his bio on Wiki, but it doesn't give much context.'

'Senator Dwayne Towers was a 24-carat asshole. However, for many of the people in my country he was a war hero, a fully paid-up NRA member, an anti-abortionist God-fearing Christian WASP, a Trump acolyte, and an all-round great guy. His father was state governor and then a congressman. He therefore came from a minor political dynasty. In Vietnam, he was a fighter ace. He fitted the Trump hero criteria in that he never got captured. Back then he was known as "The Teflon Kid". Nothing stuck to him in 'Nam. All the accusations of napalming a loyal village, shooting down a bomber in a friendly-fire incident, or whoring with underage hookers, never stuck to Captain Towers. No siree!'

Nacho noted that Zinczenko's face had darkened as he spoke about the Senator. It was clear that the journalist would not give him an unbiased opinion of the politician. Meanwhile, Zinczenko was continuing.

'Then, when Towers became a senator, the same thing happens. He evolves into "The Teflon Senator". The accusations of corruption to secure contracts for factories in his state, all those overseas fact-finding junkets paid for by foreign governments, the underage daughters of donors, the help from foreign hackers to secure re-election! Nothing stuck to Senator Towers. His voting base loved him all the more, the more outrageous he became. Racism, bigotry, and anti-Semitism are not just the purview of rednecks and trailer trash, but exist across the whole of our society. So, Towers was elected, time after time.'

'Yes, I gathered from what I read that he was quite right wing.'

'Quite right wing? Quite right wing! This guy made Attila the Hun look like fucking Karl Marx. But it got worse. Lately, people have been talking about him as Trump's successor in the 2024 election. In fact, the rumour is that Trump actually thought about him as his vice-president in 2016, but was persuaded that a ticket of "Trump-Towers" was a step too far in advertising his own corporation, even for Trump. Trump Towers! Get it? So, instead Trump picked the cardboard cut-out that is Mike Pence.'

'Do you really think he would have been a candidate in 2024? I mean, by then he would have been in his late seventies.'

'Sure, why not? Trump is nearly seventy-four and would be seventy-eight if he completes a second term. Bernie Saunders is seventy-eight, Joe Biden is seventy-seven, Michael Bloomberg is also seventy-eight. We Americans seem to like old white guys leading us. Obama and Kennedy were exceptions. Towers had got the right politics to inherit Trump's base. He was forever on cable news and shock-jock shows as a surrogate for the President. One GOP official put it to me that he was even better than Trump. At least he wasn't an alleged draft dodger. My contact said Towers was "Trump without the bone spurs".'

'I met his wife, Miriam Towers. I was told she was distraught when she heard the news, yet when I showed her the body, she seemed quite calm, more disappointed than upset.'

'Oh, I imagine she was distraught and disappointed all right, but not because dear old Dwayne had died. Miriam Towers is a sort of Lady Macbeth.'

'Ah, the "Scottish play".'

'You know your Shakespeare?'

'My mother was an English teacher. I was given a copy of Lambs' *Tales from Shakespeare* when I went to primary school, aged six, and then she gave me *The Complete Works* when I went to high school at fifteen. I must confess I read the former, but not the latter.'

'Well, I was an English major at SUNY, and we did a lot of the Bard in our curriculum.'

'SUNY?'

'State University of New York. Now, Inspector, if you know your *Macbeth*, you'll know that his wife is a scheming, ambitious bitch. The Washington rumour mill is that Miriam had her sights firmly set on being America's First Lady. It's why she put up with his aforementioned peccadilloes. Although Towers came from a fairly well-to-do family, they were not that rich. He married Miriam and married into money. Her father owned Paradise Pickets, the fence company. They made pre-painted white picket fences for middle-class America by the mile. Every decent home had a white picket fence around its yard. Realtors insisted on it if you wanted a house sale. It was as American as apple pie. Her old man made a mint.

47

Originally, they used wood, but switched to plastic in the sixties, and continued to rack up millions,' said Zinczenko, and then he burst into song with a tuneless jingle. 'Pick Paradise Pickets for your paradise.'

'Doesn't sound like a Billboard Number One.'

'No, but it's irritating enough to have gotten into the head of lots of fence-buying Americans. It was on in commercial breaks on TV most nights for decades and in prime slots, like the Super Bowl.'

'Often the murderer is someone close to the victim, often a relative in fact, but what you're saying is that it's unlikely his wife ordered a hit on Towers, as her ambition would have been thwarted.'

'Exactly.'

'One thing I don't understand is why Senator Towers didn't have a security detail?'

'Outside of the President, the Veep, and their families, only the Speaker and the party leaders of the two Houses get security. Otherwise, senators and representatives are on their own. They have to go private, although of course their local state often chips in. Anyway, Towers is down here at "The End of the World". Who's going to hurt him down here in the middle of nowhere? His visit to Torres del Paine wasn't part of his official schedule either, so it would be difficult to plan an assassination, which means you're looking at a crime of opportunity. Somebody got to him, I'm convinced!'

'And do you have anyone in mind for this crime, if indeed you're correct and Senator Towers was murdered, rather than died of natural causes?'

'Well, from the little I've picked up, Towers seemed okay when he left here and he must have been okay to hike five miles across hill and dale in strong winds to reach where he died. So, my guess is that one of my fellow countrymen, or indeed countrywomen, did the deed. Your job, Inspector, is to find out which one.'

'Maybe you can give me background on the other Americans on the hike?'

'Sure, why not?'

CHAPTER 7

Zinczenko went over to his laptop and pulled up a document on the screen before speaking. 'Let's see, I've already made some notes here. I gather quite a few of the guests were really pissed when Towers showed up and joined the TripLux party. A few have said if they'd known he was on it, they wouldn't have come. Here we are. Ladies first? "For the female of the species is deadlier than the male".'

'Kipling?'

'Yes, I believe so. You really are well read.'

'For a dumb Chilean cop, you mean?'

'I've learned never to underestimate the cops, Inspector. I've given voice anonymously to many of them in my time who would have been fired or worse if they'd been caught talking to a journalist. Now, first up is Taylor Burroughs. She's an influencer and top-ranked Instababe.'

'She's a what?'

'An "influencer". She specialises in travel. She has an Instagram account and a blog with hundreds of thousands of followers. She's what's known as an "Instababe" – a queen of social media. She can influence so many people that companies ply her with clothes and stuff to show and talk about on her accounts as she travels the world. Product placement it's called. Everything from suntan oil to suitcases.

Then the travel companies get her to take their tours for nothing, or the airlines give her free passage, usually at the front of the plane. I'll bet TripLux have given her this trip for free. Now, she and Towers did have a Twitter spat a few months ago after she went on a trip to his state. Seems like she didn't enjoy it. She compared the people there to the inbreds in the film *Deliverance*.'

'I don't think I've seen that one.'

'You haven't? Duelling banjoes? No? Well, you should download it, it's a great movie. However, I don't think an argument on Twitter is reason enough to kill someone.'

'Probably not,' agreed Nacho.

'Next up is Hester Wilson. Now, she's an interesting lady. Her sister claimed she was sexually assaulted by Dwayne Towers at a fundraiser her parents were hosting for Towers' father. They were major donors to Towers Senior. The sister was underage and became pregnant. Nobody believed her charges against Towers, not her own parents, not the press, and certainly not the cops. They all thought the baby's father was some school friend that she was trying to protect and that her accusation was just a way of getting back at her parents. She was allegedly a bit of a stroppy teenager at the time. Back in the day, given the laws then in place, she was forced to have the baby, but the baby died during childbirth. No blood tests at the time. And since the baby was cremated, no opening of the coffin to test for DNA when that technology came along later. In the meantime, the sister committed suicide.'

'Sounds quite a tragedy,' said Nacho. 'How did the sister who's here react?'

'Badly. She's Ms Wilson and has never married. Seems to hate men, but isn't gay either. Hester Wilson has been after Towers since she inherited her daddy's millions. She's pro-abortion and supports a string of pregnancy advice clinics. She'd certainly have access to drugs via those clinics if Towers died of poisoning. And then last, but by no means least, amongst the females, there's Hollywood legend Miranda Alexandra.'

'Ah, yes, one of my adolescent favourites. Why would she have wanted to kill Senator Towers?'

'Because she hated him? That a good enough reason? Miranda always has been politically active. She was an ardent anti-war protestor against Vietnam. She's famous for bearing her breasts at a Capitol sit-in back then and for handcuffing herself to the railings outside the White House, as well as for other stunts. Over time she's turned vegan, became a gym bunny with a string of Pilates videos, endorsed the anti-fur lobby, and is now a climate activist.'

'If she's a climate activist, why is she flying around on a TripLux private jet?'

'I asked her that question the other day. She said she wanted to see all these cultural and natural wonders so she could understand better how they needed to be protected, and that this tour was the most efficient in terms of carbon emissions. Seems a bit flimsy to me.'

'You said she hated Towers?'

'Yeah. Towers played his Vietnam vet card frequently in elections and derided her as a traitor. He used her as an example of all that was wrong with what he called the loony left. Then he also brought up her past history of losing husbands. "To lose one husband may be regarded as misfortune, to lose a second looks like carelessness".'

'That's a parody on Oscar Wilde. Is this some sort of English test, Mr Zinczenko?'

'Not at all. I'm sorry if it seems that way. Miranda lost her first husband, her co-star in many films, Peter March, to a drug overdose. Rumour in Tinseltown was that it wasn't self-administered as they'd been having marriage difficulties for some months. Nevertheless, the official verdict was that the OD was self-inflicted.'

'You said "husbands", plural.'

'I did indeed. A few years later, she loses another husband, the Hollywood mogul, Robert Dorr, the man who helped her win her Oscar. He was poisoned. Again, this came after much gossip about strains in their marriage. This time the Filipina cook took the rap, although she declared her innocence, and she's still inside declaring it to this day. And again, the rumour mill speculated that Miranda may have been the real guilty party. You see, her dad was a pharmacist and she worked in his drugstore in her teens. The story goes, apocryphal I'm sure, that the area around the store was littered with dead cats, dogs, raccoons and other critters that Miranda experimented on. But then she became a teenage beauty, Hollywood beckoned, and her publicists have brushed all that under the carpet.'

'Very interesting. I hadn't heard any of that. Her publicists have been quite successful.'

'Yes, and if anybody brings any of this up, she'll slap a writ on them as fast as you can sneeze.'

'What about the men on the hike?'

'Well, first, there's Randy Thompson, the drag queen. He has his own TV show in California. Have you seen it? It's called *The American Queen*. He's very camp, very flamboyant, and on stage, very funny. However, off it, he's a serious campaigner for LGBT rights. Towers was, of course, anti-LGBT. Got to keep the voting base happy. Towers blocked LGBT legislation in the Senate which would have given more protection to gay couples. He and Thompson had some nasty exchanges and almost came to physical blows on a shared platform on one of the late-night talk shows. There was certainly no love lost between them.'

'Senator Towers seemed to pick a lot of fights,' observed Nacho.

'You don't know the half of it yet. Randy is here with his partner, Gabriel. This one is no angel though. In an apparent act of charity, Randy picked Gabriel out from some *favela* in Rio when he was just a teenager. His family had migrated to the big city from the Amazon rainforest. He's also Randy's minder, and has had several scuffles with the paparazzi protecting his partner's privacy. One photographer ended up with a broken leg, and another with cracked ribs. Those incidents, and maybe others we've not heard about, were settled out of court with the snappers getting a tidy sum of cash. Their latest line in money-spinning is a series of fitness and grooming videos aimed at the LGBT market. I've seen some stills, and both men are built like bodybuilders under all those sequins and pantyhose.'

'Thanks. And then there should be one more?'

'Yes, finally, there's Muhammad Ismail. Mo, as he prefers to be known, is a Somali immigrant turned US citizen. He's one of Silicon Valley's brightest stars. A Stanford graduate who's developed a whole series of apps. You've probably got some of them on your phone or tablet. Now he's into artificial intelligence. He's also very generous; a real philanthropist. Mo's also politically active. He's pro-immigration, anti-wall, and he led the civil activist groups that pressured the Ninth Circuit Court of Appeals to restrain Trump's first travel ban. He and Towers have clashed on the issue with op eds in the press. Now, the interesting rumour about Mo is that, back in Somalia, he was a child soldier before he was rehabilitated and came to the US. He's been a trained killer from a very young age.'

'I see,' said Nacho slowly, remembering Hugo's assertion that Ismail and Towers had a heated argument the previous day.

'So, you see, Inspector, for whatever reason, several of those on the hike with Towers had a reason to dislike him at best, hate him at worst, and have suspicious deaths in their histories. Could Towers be one more?'

'Right, thank you, Mr Zinczenko, you've given me useful background for my interviews with each of the hikers. Now, do you know anything about the other two participants. Henderson and Sullivan?'

'No, they're not Americans. They're from countries far away from Towers' world. Why would they want to kill a US senator?'

'Agreed, it seems unlikely.'

'I'm afraid it's like one of those country house mysteries so beloved of British thriller writers.'

'Ah, you mean Agatha Christie, G. K. Chesterton, Dorothy Sayers and so on. I used to read those to help develop my English. I liked trying to solve the crimes before the end of the book. Maybe that's why I became a real-life detective,' said Nacho with a smile as the two men shook hands.

'Exactly. Each person has a credible means, motive and opportunity.'

'Based on what you've said, Mr Zinczenko, each certainly had the motive. The means, I've narrowed down to two possibilities. But the opportunity is still a puzzle. The Senator seems to have taken ill in front of eight witnesses and died alone, isolated in a wooden hut. Not so much a grand English country house, but more a small Chilean public toilet. Now that really is a mystery. Thanks again and goodbye for now, Señor.'

'I hope you'll keep me posted on your investigation.'

'I'll see what I can do, but I can't promise anything. You know that, with your experience.'

'Sure, I know. Goodbye, Inspector. And since you like reading in English, why not buy a copy of *Death of a Dream*. It's available at all good bookstores, and Amazon of course.'

'Of course,' said Nacho and he left.

CHAPTER 8

Mindful that he needed to wrap the case up as soon as possible, Nacho arranged for each of the hikers to come and see him in the meeting room in the hotel conference centre after dinner. He asked the front desk to tell the specific guests about their appointments that evening and left it to the receptionists to sort out the order.

He gave the desk a letter to deliver to each hiker. In the letter, Nacho explained his regrets at having to schedule the interviews after a long day and such a traumatic experience, but that he was sure that they'd appreciate that the death of a US senator was a serious matter that warranted urgent investigation. He emphasised that under the circumstances, since lawyers would not be present, and the interviews not taped, that anything said could not be used in court and that attendance was voluntary. He also warned them that they should refrain from sharing anything about their interviews, or any speculation around Senator Towers' demise, with the media or anyone else, on penalty of prosecution under Chilean law. Nacho had made the last bit up, but was pretty sure that none of the interviewees would check, as it sounded official.

Before the interviews, Nacho googled each person's name and made notes. There were some surprising additions to Zinczenko's summaries and information at last on the Englishman and the

Australian. He also ran a check on the National Criminal Records site for Andrés Bravo, the concierge.

The first hiker to be interviewed was Hester Wilson. She proved to be the lady of indeterminate age in Hugo's photograph. She was petite, wore glasses that gave her a serious, stern look, and had short blonde hair, obviously dyed. Nacho had to endure a tirade against Senator Towers and all he stood for before his interviewee launched into a polemic about the right-wing suborning of the US Supreme Court, and the risk that the landmark "Roe vs. Wade" ruling on abortion could be overturned. When she had finally finished, Nacho felt able to begin the interview.

'Now, Ms Wilson, from a photograph your guide took yesterday at lunchtime you were sitting with the other ladies, Ms Burroughs and Ms Alexandra, some way from the Senator.'

'That's correct. I wouldn't want to breathe in any oxygen atoms that bastard may have used.'

'And did you at any time during the day walk beside the Senator?'

'And what, slip him a Mickey Finn? No, I did not. I kept as far away from that monster as possible. I'm not saying that I didn't spend my time fantasising about skewering him with my walking pole, or pushing him overboard from the catamaran, but I did not murder that sonofabitch, even though he deserved it. And before you ask me, yes, I'm glad he's dead. Do you know what that man did to my fifteen-year-old sister?'

'Yes, Ms Wilson, I have read about the accusation, but as far as I'm aware, nothing was proven.'

'Nothing was proven because the baby died and was cremated before any blood tests to prove paternity could be taken. All arranged by Towers' father, no doubt.'

'Look, I'm sorry about your sister, Ms Wilson, I really am, but I can't do anything about that. Now, may we return to yesterday's events? As far as I know, Senator Towers may have died of a heart attack or other natural causes. We won't know for sure until there's been an autopsy. However, one possibility is that Senator Towers was poisoned. Obviously, you and he didn't get along, to put it mildly. So, I have to ask you, do you have access to drugs at the abortion clinics you run?'

'They're pregnancy advisory clinics, actually. We help underage girls and poorer women through their pregnancies, but yes, we do abortions there if the mother-to-be decides that's what she wants. We firmly believe that it's a woman's right to choose. Some of the terminations are medication abortions, but while they obviously cause the pregnancy to end, the mother is unharmed. Even if I wanted to poison Towers – and that's just one of the ways I've thought about killing him in my daydreams – the drugs at our clinics are not suitable.'

After a few more questions, Nacho decided that Hester Wilson was unlikely to have been the culprit. She certainly had the motive given her heated rhetoric towards the Senator, but it was difficult to see the opportunity, or access to a method which wasn't witnessed by others.

Nacho's second interview was with Taylor Burroughs. He could immediately see why she was a social media hit. She was in her late twenties, extremely pretty, with almond-shaped eyes, high cheekbones, a mixed-race complexion, and long, lustrous dark hair. She was smartly dressed in the best outdoor clothing brands, but made them look like the most sophisticated catwalk fashion. He was sure many of her followers would want to look like her and do whatever she did with whatever products she claimed were the best. Her job seemed to be that of a walking-billboard freeloader, the perfect virtual poster girl for rich millennials who celebrated looks over substance. However, after a short period in her company he came to the conclusion that if Taylor Burroughs had murdered anyone, she would have blogged about it within half an hour, endorsing whichever brand of gun, knife or poison she had used.

'Thank you for your time, Señorita.'

'Mmm, Señorita! I like the way you say it. It sounds so sexy. If you want to say some more sexy things to me, I'm in room 18,' she said in a husky voice, dripping with innuendo.

Nacho thought that if he took up this offer, his performance would probably be rated and placed on the Internet along with a compromising picture.

'Thank you, Ms Burroughs, but I'll have to work late tonight. Good evening.'

His next interview was with Miranda Alexandra. Nacho found himself sweating. He'd never been with a Hollywood star before, much less an Oscar winner, and a frequent cast member of his teenage fantasies. When she entered the room, rather than smelling of fragrant perfume as he'd expected, she smelled of alcohol. His suspicion that the actor was drunk was confirmed the minute she spoke, and she slurred her words throughout the interview. All that aside, she was still stunningly beautiful at nearly seventy years old, although Nacho wasn't sure how much of that was due to cosmetic surgery. After the preliminaries, during which the star kept touching Nacho on the arm while looking into his eyes, Nacho focused on some tougher questions.

'Now, Ms Alexandra, I gather you and Senator Towers have a history of enmity?'

'Please, call me Miranda,' said the movie star, pawing him once more.

'Thank you, but please can you answer the question, Miranda?'

'Yes, our mutual hate goes back a long way. We never agreed on anything. Vietnam, women's rights, hunting, the environment. You name it, we disagreed about it.'

'And at the lunch, you were some way from the Senator when he took ill?'

'Yes, me and the other gals sat as far from him as possible. He was well known for his wandering hands. Even in these days of #MeToo he had a reputation as an incorrigible molester. Not that abusing women is seen as a bad thing for GOP politicians these days, especially by the so-called evangelicals.'

'And did you walk beside the Senator at any stage on the hike? Share any snacks with him?'

'Share snacks with him?' asked Ms Alexandra, her voice full of indignation. 'I wouldn't piss on that bastard if he was on fire, much less share anything with him. Wait a minute, do you think I might have poisoned him? Have you been reading all those scurrilous stories about me? They're all lies, you know. Making out as if I'm a sort of black widow preying on husbands. You go down that route and I'll have you and your Chilean police force sued for false accusations; don't you worry.'

Nacho thought that one minute the actor seemed to have been hitting on him, and now it looked like she wanted to literally hit him. She had switched from cougar to diva in seconds.

'I'm not accusing you of anything, Señora. I'm just trying to find out what happened to Senator Towers.'

'Well, I'm not saying anything more without my attorney being present. Good day.'

The movie star got up and flounced out, leaving Nacho to wonder if she had been acting during her histrionics to put him off pursuing her reputation about her husbands' deaths, or if it was the wine talking and she was just too drunk.

If he discounted the influencer, Nacho thought the other two women may be potential poisoners, but on the other hand, they were remote from Towers when the Senator upped and went to the toilet. *Maybe the men in the party will offer more clues*, he thought.

CHAPTER 9

Nacho moved on to the next interviewee, Callum Henderson. Although, up until now, everyone referred to him as English, Nacho's research had revealed that Henderson was in fact a Scot. Nacho seemed to remember that this sort of thing mattered to people from Britain for some reason. From his web search, he had learned that Henderson was a former British Army officer, a veteran of the Falklands War, and was now a defence contractor with a drone company. His product was designed to seek out enemy troop concentrations from on high, and then automatically dive on them, before exploding into a fireball. It was nicknamed the "Kamikaze Drone".

Nacho had also learned that Henderson's company, Defence Drones Limited, or DDL, had lost a contract with the US Army after the Senate Armed Services Committee had revisited the tendering procedure. The need to keep the development of drone technology in the US, even if DDL was from an allied country, was cited as the reason for the review. The committee was chaired at the time by Senator Towers. Intriguingly, the contract had been reassigned to a manufacturer in Towers' own state. DDL had lost millions of pounds in stock value, with Henderson as the major stockholder. Since Henderson was now in his early sixties, Nacho surmised that this must have been a major blow to the ex-soldier's pension pot.

Henderson was taller than Nacho remembered from the hike, probably close to 1.9 metres, and he looked extremely fit for his age, with muscles bulging under his blue T-shirt. The man sported a military haircut, was suntanned, and overall was the picture of health. Fleetingly, Nacho hoped that he would look like this when he was fifty, never mind sixty.

After the introductory preliminaries, Nacho got down to business with Henderson. 'Can you tell me why you're here in Torres del Paine, Mr Henderson?'

'I was in the area and knew about the park by reputation, so I decided to drive up from Punta Arenas to see if its reputation is deserved. And, I must say, scenically, it is.'

'What were you doing in Punta Arenas?'

'I'd flown over from the Falkland Islands. I fought there in 1982 against the Argentinians. Back then I was a young lieutenant in the SAS – they're our special forces. One of our operations had been to try to get at the Argentinian fighters based at Río Grande on Tera del Fuego. "Operation Mikado" it was called. The Argies' Exocet missiles were causing havoc with our fleet, and we wanted to eliminate the aircraft launching them. I was part of a team sent in to do a recce on their airbase. The mission had to be aborted due to bad weather and our helicopter was abandoned near Punta Arenas. So, in answer to your question, I was reliving the experience, forty years on. Probably my last visit.'

'Did you know Senator Towers?'

'Not personally, no. I knew of him.'

'Would that be due to his role on the Armed Services Committee and its cancellation of your company's contract to supply drones to the American Army?'

'Yes, that's correct.'

'And how did you feel about Senator Towers after that?'

'I didn't feel anything in particular. In fact, if anything, I admired the man. He'd fought in Vietnam, he'd defended jobs on his turf, and he was a patriotic sort. Nothing there I could disagree with. I wish some British politicians had balls like him. His actions weren't personal. You have to move on.'

'But losing that contract caused your company millions, and indeed, you lost a substantial amount yourself as a major shareholder when the stock plummeted.'

'True, but one thing I learned in the Regiment, Inspector, is that if at first you don't succeed, try, try, and try again. If you're thinking of using that financial disaster as a motive for me to kill Senator Towers, then you need to think again. I've killed many people in my life, Inspector, but Towers wasn't one of them. Anyway, DDL is very much a viable company once more. We're just about to announce a major order from Turkey, and we're setting up licensed production there in the near future. I expect our share price will rebound upon us releasing the news. So, no sweat, Inspector, I'll be independently wealthy once more. I had no need to avenge myself on Towers.'

Henderson had remained cool throughout Nacho's questioning. After the ex-soldier left, Nacho speculated to himself that the man's special forces' training had included resisting interrogation.

Nacho's next interview was with the Australian, Jim Sullivan. Sullivan was the r-E-source mining company CEO and a self-made billionaire – at least in Australian dollars. There was little on the web about him that Nacho could find, other than some press statements about how protective he was about his privacy. There seemed to be general amazement that he had never taken his company public, and that it was still unlisted on the ASX, the Australian Stock Exchange. The press seemed equally surprised that his deputy was a female, and the coverage seemed to reflect a heavy male bias in the Australian corporate world. The little history available showed that Sullivan had been born in Melbourne, flew for a period with the Royal Australian Air Force, done a mining engineering degree at Monash University, and eventually set up his own company. This had gone on to be hugely successful and he was now one of Australia's richest citizens, if not the richest. Although historically a very private person, it was noted that Sullivan had recently taken to speaking out on environmental issues and the rights of Australia's indigenous peoples. One article in Nacho's web search mentioned that for a man who usually shunned publicity, Sullivan had uncharacteristically decided to sponsor a Formula-E electric racing car team.

The Australian proved to be a completely bald, leathery-skinned, small and wiry individual. Nacho was surprised at the baldness, but realised that he'd only seen the man earlier in the day with a woolly hat on. The man spoke with a broad Australian accent, and, with his firm grip, he almost crushed Nacho's fingers when they shook hands.

'I gather you're a mining company CEO, Mr Sullivan. I hope you don't have any designs on Torres del Paine, Señor,' said Nacho, trying some humour to put the foreigner at ease.

'This is the last place I'd look to mine, Inspector. Sounds like you don't know too much about r-E-source?'

'No, I don't, other than its curious name and logo.'

'Well, the "E" is in upper case because that's what my company's about. "E" for electrification! I believe that by 2050, less than half of our direct-use energy will come from fossil fuels and the rest will be from electricity. That's what I've bet the company on, anyway. We specialise in mining the main metal ores needed for electrification, and preferably for renewable generation. In the future, we expect excess energy to be stored in industrial-scale batteries. We mine copper, aluminium, lithium, cobalt, and the rare earths. That's how I got to know Chile so well. We have copper and lithium mines here, up in the Atacama. I employ several thousand of your countrymen I'm proud to say. And we do it at a decent wage, with good accommodation at the mine sites, and an excellent safety record. Our mine sites run on solar and wind power supported by battery banks. All the light vehicles are electrics or hybrids, and we've just received our first 290-ton electric ore-moving truck. She's a whopper!'

The man's enthusiasm shone through and Nacho was impressed by what he'd heard. It sounded good for Chile, the economy, and the workers. The Australian continued, 'And, more than that, it's written into our company articles that when the sites are exhausted of ore, they'll be reclaimed as well as technology allows, the tailings ponds will be remediated, and the whole lot turned over as a gift to your government as national parks.'

'Wow, that's very impressive, Mr Sullivan. On behalf of Chile, I can only say thank you.' Nacho thought he was grovelling a bit as he said this. He hated grovelling.

'No worries, Inspector. We're doing the same elsewhere. Back home, my company's giving land back to the indigenous peoples of Australia, to the Aborigines as they were known. I'm afraid we white men stole it from them. In fact, I was learning that the same thing happened here, too. How do you say it – the Tehuelche people? – they suffered a similar fate here, didn't they? Sounds like they had a pretty grim time at the hands of Europeans. I saw some of their cave paintings the last time I visited over on the east side of the park.'

'Isn't it unusual for someone in your line of work to be so concerned about historical land ownership of the previous inhabitants?' asked Nacho, curious at the man's seemingly boundless philanthropy.

'Maybe, but you see, I had a daughter, Katy. She became very interested in indigenous peoples' rights. That, and my focus on my company, meant we became a little estranged. Then she was killed in a car crash. At her funeral, hundreds of indigenous people turned out. I had no idea she was held in such high esteem by them. I talked to the tribal elders and found out more about what she had been doing, and as I did so, I had a sort of epiphany. I swore on that day I'd try in some small way to use my wealth and company resources to help roll back some of the historic wrongs. So, no, I can safely say I have no designs on Torres del Paine, other than to be a frequent visitor, as it's a magical place.'

'Thank you again, Mr Sullivan, I fully agree with you. Now, I know it's just a formality, but I have to ask you a few questions. Did you know Senator Towers?'

'No, I'd never met the man before we went on the hike.'

'Have you had any business dealings in America where your company might have come across him?'

'No, can't say we have. We have several customers in the US who take our products for making into power cables, transformers and other grid equipment. Our lithium sells well to the gigafactories of the big battery manufacturers up there. We've also got research going on at some of the American universities on recycling. I want our mines to ultimately reduce capacity and become more sustainable.'

'That doesn't sound like a good business model, if I may say so,' said Nacho, thinking back to his university economics course. 'Surely you'll be putting yourself out of business?'

'That's one advantage of owning a private company, Inspector. I don't have to worry about shareholders and I don't need any more money. And, as our mines reduce in size, we'll retrain our operatives to become manufacturers of what's needed for the green economy.'

'Impressive. And while doing all this, are you sure you never came across Senator Towers? He was quite involved in American energy matters I believe, but as an advocate for coal and oil.'

'As I've already said, Inspector, I can't say I ever came across him personally, and I can't say I've heard from my American managers about Senator Towers ever getting involved directly in our business. However, we're a large company, and maybe one of our people knew him. Now, I do know he wasn't a supporter of the Green New Deal and was a bit of a dinosaur on energy matters, supporting the coal lobby and the oil companies as you've said, but we've not spoken to him directly, as far as I know.'

'At the lunch, yesterday, Mr Sullivan, you sat next to the Senator. How did he seem to you?'

'Fine, he seemed fine. Then he got up abruptly and said he had to go to the john. It was as if he had stomach cramps or something. You know how it is if you get the shits? He sped off into one of the chemical dunnies.'

'Did you see anyone else visit the – what did you call them? – "dunnies"?'

'I think that Thompson and Mo Ismail went as well. I know Thompson went off behind the huts. I'm not sure where Ismail went.'

'Okay, that will be all for now, Mr Sullivan, and thanks again for your investments in Chile.'

Nacho saw Sullivan out, and called in his next interviewee, Randy Thompson. The web search about Thompson had added little about the drag queen to what Zinczenko had told him, except the surprise that Thompson had briefly served with the US Marines. Thompson had been discharged for being overtly gay at a time when this was unacceptable in the Corps. Nacho had watched a YouTube video of the man's drag act, and could see why the butch Marines hadn't been keen on him. However, it was also clear from the viewing as to why Thompson was such a success in his chosen profession, being camp, witty, and quite beautiful when made up. He seemed to be known simply as "Randy" in the US media, another star, like Prince and Madonna, who needed only one name to be instantly recognised by the public.

Nacho's search had also added more details about Thompson's partner, Gabriel. Gabriel had come under some scrutiny after his run-ins with the paparazzi. *The press looks after its own*, Nacho thought. The media claims included one that Gabriel was a hermaphrodite, a Brazilian "she-man", as one paper put it. Another said he'd been a gangland enforcer in the *favela* he'd escaped from when lifted out of poverty by Thompson.

There were several pictures of Thompson and Gabriel on the Internet, and they were a good-looking couple. The trailer for their fitness video aimed at the LGBT community was also on the web and showed them both to have strong, sculpted physiques. In the videos their bodies were tanned, hairless, and oiled, and their tight clothing left little to the imagination. Thompson certainly looked strong enough to strangle someone. As two handsome men, one a celebrity and the other with a menacing air and a shady past, the gossip columns seemed to love following their antics. What the gossip columns didn't seem to like, was Thompson getting involved in LGBT rights. His frivolous stage persona meant some of the media couldn't take Thompson seriously, and it was this angle that Senator

Towers had apparently played on in rallies, tweets, and interviews, for the amusement of his voting base.

One article Nacho found had a link to the video clip of Thompson and Towers on the chat show that Zinczenko had mentioned. In it, Thompson had lunged at the Senator, and the guest in between, a burly ex-bodybuilding film star, had intervened to keep them apart. The look of hate on Thompson's face had been a sight, and Nacho was pretty sure that, given the right opportunity, Thompson could have killed the Senator. He decided to focus on this in the interview once the preliminaries were out of the way.

'Now, Mr Thompson, I gather that you and Senator Towers were not on good terms?'

'That's putting it mildly,' replied Thompson, grimacing at the mention of Towers' name.

Nacho was surprised. For some reason he had expected Thompson to speak with the effeminate voice of a female impersonator like his stage persona, but instead, the man spoke in a deep and resonant voice.

'And I've seen at least one instance where you physically tried to attack the Senator.'

'You mean on *The Witching Hour* talk show? He goaded me and I let my control slip. I vowed that day to never lose control again. I also vowed to get even.'

'You didn't face any charges or a law suit from the Senator?'

'My lawyers made it quite clear to his attorneys, that if Towers wanted a show trial to boost his ratings with his base, and weaponise my sexuality against me, we would bring up his sexual history as well. That would include past accusations about him and underage girls. In preparation for the fight, some private detectives we'd hired found out about some juicy pay-offs and non-disclosure agreements that various young ladies – and I mean *very* young ladies – had signed after relationships with Towers. We let his lawyers know about this, and they quickly backed down. It's an election year, after all!'

'I've also seen the trailer for your new fitness video. You and your partner appear to be in good physical shape in it. The trailer shows you lifting considerable weights and in one exercise you squeeze a grapefruit until it bursts, so I know you have strong hands, Mr Thompson. Now I gather that during the lunch on the hike yesterday that you sat next to the Senator, despite your hatred of him?'

'There was nowhere else to sit. We were all sitting on stones to keep our butts dry and the one behind Towers was the only one left when I got there. Believe me, if I'd known he was going to be here, or on the hike, I'd never have bothered.'

'I also gather that you were in the US Marines?'

'What's that got to do with anything? Ah, I get it, you think I'm some sort of trained killer,' said Thompson and he laughed. 'Well, I never made it past officers' boot camp at Quantico. The Marines didn't like gays back then. I'm not sure they really like them now. I'm surprised they even let me get that far before chucking me out.'

'Why did you join?'

'All those big strong men. What's not to like?' When he'd said this, Thompson had resorted to his stage voice, and rolled his eyes and flipped a hand, switching on the drag queen. He resorted to his natural voice before continuing. 'Yes, that's right. I took a piss and came right back. I cleaned my hands with gel the way my mommy taught me, and then finished my lunch.'

'Which hut did you use?'

'I didn't use a hut. Even in the gale that was blowing you could still smell the stink from the toilets. I just took my pecker out and peed al fresco. I'm not one of those gays who picks up guys in restrooms, you know. I've my reputation to consider!' The last sentence had been said as the drag queen once more.

'A witness saw you pass behind Senator Towers.'

'I have to confess I did. Maybe I pissed up against the hut he was using. They all looked the same.'

'There was a hole in the back of the toilet the Senator was using.'

'And, what? What are you saying? Are you saying I stuck my hands in there and strangled the bastard? Is that what you're saying?'

'I'm not saying anything, Mr Thompson, I'm only making an observation.'

'Well, I'm done with your observations. If you want to talk to me anymore, it will be with my lawyer present.'

'That will be all for now, Mr Thompson. Thank you for your time,' said Nacho to Thompson's back, as the American left the room.

The final interview was with Mo Ismail. Nacho's Internet research had shown Muhammad Ismail to be a multimillionaire Silicon Valley hotshot, who was riding the wave of the expanding digital economy. This time it seemed it was no "dot-com bubble" and he'd read that Ismail had got extremely rich, extremely quickly. The entrepreneur's fortune had developed off the back of his "Live Nurse" app, a Personal Healthcare Recording smartphone application. The app could be loaded onto a smartphone and also required a simple wristband device. Nacho had learned that the app sent a patient's data, collected via the wristband, directly to their doctor's office. The doctor pre-set various alerts for the user, depending on the patient's condition, with alarms warning the medical staff if anything untoward was happening to the phone owner. Nacho had also gleaned that, after developing a series of other apps, Ismail was now apparently expanding into artificial intelligence. He invited the digital entrepreneur to sit down.

'Well, here we are at last. Always keep the black guy waiting. Always the black guy is last. Same in Chile as at home,' said Ismail, and he shook his head.

Nacho was appalled. It had not been his intention at all, and the front desk had set up the interview schedule. He tried to sound contrite in replying to Ismail. 'I'm sorry if I've offended you in some way, Mr Ismail, but that was not my intent. Perhaps we can get straight to the point and then you can go.'

'Sounds good to me. It's been a long day today, after a trying day yesterday.'

'Yes, and I'm sorry you had to sleep on the floor of the hut last night.'

'Sleeping on the floor of that shack? Compared with how I was brought up in Somalia, that was luxury, man, luxury. I guess I slept better than any of the others, except maybe that British guy; he's a tough cookie.'

'Now, Mr Ismail, I gather you and Senator Towers have had disagreements in the past?'

'You could say that. That old dude thought that people like me shouldn't be allowed to come into his country, never mind getting citizenship. He seemed to forget the whole population were immigrants, some willing, and some unwilling. Why, even the Native Americans came over the land bridge from Asia, so in a way they're immigrants too. But, with respect to Towers, he was just a good old-fashioned racist. For him, abolition of slavery should never have happened, and the Confederate flag should be flying over the White House, instead of the Stars and Stripes.'

'Yes, I gather the Senator was anti-immigration and that you opposed him and have even funded legal fights against various actions that he and the Federal Government have taken in that area.'

'That's right. But it wasn't just the colour of my skin that Towers didn't like. I'm a Muslim, and he was anti-Islam too. I was getting ready to fund his opponent the next time he was up for re-election. Whoever killed him just saved me a bunch of cash.'

'You don't seem to be short of cash, Mr Ismail.'

'Look, it's late and I'm tired, so let me just say that I didn't kill Towers. Can I go now?'

Nacho ignored the request. 'I believe you and Senator Towers had a row out on the hike?'

'We had a very brief altercation, yes. He pushed past me and I reacted. He was irritated that I was stopping too often to take photographs. I got the impression he only liked pictures featuring himself. It was no big deal.'

'Then during the lunch yesterday, you also went to the toilet, I believe? Did you stop by the Senator's hut?'

'And what? Shoot him? Stab him? I saw his body. He wasn't shot or stabbed.'

'Where did you go?'

'I went to the hut one over from his. Look, I've just said, I didn't kill him.'

'I believe you've killed in the past, Mr Ismail.'

'That old nugget! Always comes back to bite me. Yes, I have. I killed people in Somalia. I was abducted by al-Shabaab when I was ten, trained to use an AK-47, and was shooting soldiers by the age of eleven. Luckily, I escaped and was helped to set up a new life in America. A kinder, more welcoming America than today's, I have to say. So, I do know how to shoot someone, but, as I said, I also know Towers wasn't shot.'

'You're right, Señor, he may have been strangled or poisoned.'

'Ah, so you think I went on to the dark web and sourced some Wabayo or something, do you?'

'What's Wabayo, Señor?' asked Nacho, confused. It sounded like a Chinese takeaway noodle house.

'Arrow-tip poison, used in Somalia by native hunters. From the Wabei tree roots. Look, it doesn't matter. Listen, Inspector, if I'd wanted to destroy Towers, I'd have taken him down by digital means. I would have hacked into his computers and found out every detail of his tax dodges, his bribes, and his sexual preferences, and I would have made sure the FBI and the IRS swarmed all over him like a cheap suit. He would have been finished as a politician and spent the last years of his life in a federal prison. And, sure, I've even thought about doing exactly that. But, thinking about it isn't the same as doing it. And anyways, I'd have made it look like it was done by the Russians, the Chinese or the North Koreans. Anybody but me. That's what I would have done to finish off Towers. Now, is that all, Inspector?'

'That will do for now, Mr Ismail. Thank you.'

CHAPTER 10

Nacho had just switched off the lights in the meeting room and stepped into the corridor when he was verbally assailed by a large woman dressed all in black with lank hair to match. The harridan had a TripLux logo on the polo shirt stretched across her ample bosom. Her broad backside and tree-trunk thighs were poured into skin-tight leggings. Overall, it wasn't a good look, thought Nacho before her voice grated into his ear.

'Are you the policeman who's harassing our guests? Don't you think they've been through enough? Can't you see that they're tired? How dare you pester them when they've all been through the trauma of seeing their friend dead. And poor Mrs Towers! You've even bothered her, too. How unthoughtful can you be?'

'Whoa, wait a minute, Miss…?'

'Sarah Spicer. I'm the TripLux rep. There's a rumour that you think Senator Towers may have been murdered and that he didn't die of natural causes? Well, thank God for that.'

'Why do you say that, Señorita?'

'Because it means the company cannot be blamed. And it means our policy of guests self-certifying they're fit can remain in place. We'll get enough bad publicity as it is for taking a guest to somewhere they can be assaulted, but at least we'll not be liable. I presume some

Chilean criminal has done this? Why would anyone attack such a dear man? I'm sure there will be repercussions for you and your country because of this. Allowing a VIP to be murdered in a national park run by the government. You should be ashamed of yourselves.'

'Please calm down, Ms Spicer. We don't know for sure that the Senator didn't die of a heart attack or an underlying illness. I have not concluded for certain that there was a crime yet, far less who has committed it. I do not know if it is a Chilean, or an American, or someone from another nationality, who could be involved. And that's only if he didn't die of natural causes.'

'Well, it's obviously not one of our clients who's done this, if he was murdered. They're all wealthy people from the very best backgrounds. And I suggest you tread carefully! My clients are all rich and powerful in their own ways, and they do not need this aggravation. They've come here on vacation, after all. I gather from the hotel manager that you've said that we cannot leave? Well, I have to inform you, we have a schedule to keep, and we'll be leaving tomorrow as planned. Thankfully, Senator Towers wasn't one of our party, but only a visitor here for the days at the park, so we can leave him here. Unfortunately, his poor wife will of course have to stay and be repatriated with her husband's remains.'

'No, I'm sorry, Ms Spicer, that isn't possible for two reasons. The first is that I forbid it, and, if you continue as you are, I'll arrest you personally for obstruction. And the second is that the road out of here to your aircraft at Punta Arenas is blocked, and will not be re-opened by tomorrow. So, I'm afraid you and your guests will have to wait at least until the next day, possibly later. Goodnight.'

Nacho left the dumbfounded Ms Spicer, her mouth agape, and went up to the bar. Nacho was pleased to see that he knew the barman.

'Hey, Carlos, I didn't know you were here at the Último.'

'Nacho! Good to see you, man. I heard you were around. *Inspector* Hernández now, I gather,' said the barman, throwing Nacho a mock salute. 'Yeah, I left the Explora. Got myself a promotion. I'm head barman here now.'

Carlos was preparing cocktails for two of the guests. One was having a Pisco Sour, the other a Calafate Sour, so Nacho took a bar stool to watch and asked the barman, 'Are you still peddling that old promise that if a guest drinks a Calafate Sour they're bound to come back to Torres del Paine some day?'

'Of course! How else will I keep sales up? Not to mention my tips! It pays to encourage repeat customers.'

When the barman was done and the drinks passed to a waitress, Nacho asked Carlos for a beer and was given a glass of cold draught Cristal.

'Thanks, Carlos,' said Nacho and he took a long sip. 'Phew, that tastes good after a long day. So, how does the Último compare to the Explora?'

The barman made a face. 'The pay's good, but the Explora had class – know what I mean?'

'Speaking of class, what can you tell me about the head guide around here, Fernanda?'

'Ah, the wonderful Fernanda! Beauty and brains in one neat package. But she's a little young for you, isn't she?'

'I was just interested. Policeman's curiosity, you know.'

'Policeman's curiosity, my ass! Fernanda is a great person. She's good with all the staff, never gets cross with the guests – even the stupid ones, of which we have plenty – and knows the park pretty well. I think she's from down here in Patagonia, but I forget where. Went to university in Santiago and did some college time in the States too, I believe. She was at the Explora with me. She's single, unattached – as far as I know – and far too nice a person for someone like you.'

'Thanks for the ringing endorsement, Carlos.'

'My pleasure,' said the barman, grinning. 'Always pays to be honest when the police ask you a question.' Carlos then nodded in the direction of one of the tables across the room. 'I wouldn't be playing with that guy if I was them.'

Nacho turned and recognised Sullivan, Henderson, and Dawson in a foursome playing cards, but not the final player. They were playing poker for matchsticks, which Nacho found ironic given they were all multimillionaires. Egos as well as matchsticks were at stake though, and they were playing with the intensity of powerful men used to winning.

'Which guy?' he asked Carlos.

'The Australian. I was in here the other night, and he was doing conjuring tricks. He made people's watches disappear and turn up in someone else's pocket. He made a 500-peso coin vanish and then pulled it out from behind someone's ear. He's very good at it. I daresay he's quick with those playing cards, too.'

'He seems an okay guy though?'

'Yeah, he's a generous tipper. Unlike the guy opposite him, Dawson. He's a mean bastard, if you'll excuse my language. Look at him. Thinks he's Paul Newman in *The Sting*.'

The pile of matchsticks in front of Dawson was depleted compared with his peers, and Nacho was perversely pleased that the oilman was losing.

'Mind you, if I was playing in that game, I'd give all my matches to the English guy,' said Carlos.

'Why's that?'

'He warned the others before they sat down that he's a sore loser. It's rumoured he's ex-military. One of the maids saw him in the spa and was waxing lyrical about his six-pack. Seems like he keeps himself in shape. She claimed he looked like Daniel Craig in his Speedos.'

Just then, Fernanda came into the bar and joined Nacho and Carlos. 'Did you just say Nacho looks like Daniel Craig in his Speedos?' she asked.

'You wish,' said Carlos, and they all laughed.

'Hi, I've been looking for you,' Fernanda said to Nacho.

'Oh, why?'

'Just thought it would be nice to keep a stranger company.'

'Would you like a beer?'

'Sorry, we're not allowed to drink alcohol in front of the guests. House rules.'

'I didn't realise I was a guest.'

'You're not, but there are real guests around. Do you want to come over to my room? I've got beers down there.'

'At the end of a long day, what could be better than a beer in a beautiful lady's bedroom.'

'Don't get any ideas, Nacho, I'm only offering beer,' she said and set off.

'Right now, it's the best offer I've got,' muttered Nacho, winking at Carlos, who smiled and shook his head. As Nacho passed the card players, Dawson called out.

'Hey, it's Corn Chip, the detective. You figured out how poor old Dwayne died yet, son?'

'I'm not at liberty to disclose the state of my inquiries to members of the public, Mr Dawson.'

'Who's this?' asked the fourth card player that Nacho didn't know. He sounded like an extra from a bad spaghetti western.

'This here young guy is who the Chilean police have sent to clear up how Dwayne died,' explained Dawson, shaking his head, as if in disbelief, as he said it.

'Hmm, he don't look like no Colombo, that's for sure,' said the unknown man.

'And who, may I ask, are you, Señor?'

'I'm Winston Harvey,' replied the man as if Nacho should know the name.

'You know, "The Tractor King"?' added Dawson.

'No, I don't know. I don't own a tractor and have no intention of buying one. So, do you have anything of value to add to my inquiry, Mr Harvey?'

'No, only that Dwayne Towers was a good man. He'd certainly make and keep America great.'

'Yes, you were right, Mr Harvey, you had nothing of value to add, goodnight.'

As Nacho turned on his heel, Nacho saw Henderson winking at him and Sullivan was grinning.

'Jesus, some of these old guys,' muttered Nacho when he caught up with Fernanda.

'You know the old guiding rule, Nacho. When you get assholes like him, you just smile and then take them up the steepest trail you can find to give them a bit of a workout, and then enjoy their huffing and puffing. Music to the ears.'

'Is that what Hugo did to Towers?'

'That's not what I meant and you know it.'

'Yes, I do know. Whatever else he was, the Senator seems to have been a fit seventy-year-old. Come on, let's get that beer.'

CHAPTER 11

'So, how come you went from being a guide in the park to being a policeman?' asked Fernanda, as she opened two Australis lagers. She handed one to Nacho and they drank from the bottles.

'My dad lost his job on the railways due to the corruption of his bosses and/or politicians. I decided to study economics at university with the idea of joining the police to fight that sort of thing. However, I ended up in homicide. Then, one of my investigations got a little bit hot politically, and I was sent down here until things cooled down. Now, it's my turn. How come you have such a strange surname?'

'MacLeod? It's a Scottish name. Some of my ancestors were from a place called Stornoway, over there. They came to Patagonia as sheep farmers and eventually married into Chilean-Spanish stock. Then the sheep farmers were driven off by the cattle barons, and so they went into meat packing. My father still loved the land though, and I guess he passed it on to me. So, after studying ecology at university in Santiago and California, I came here as a guide. I love being outdoors, and I love Torres del Paine.'

'Yes, it kind of gets to you, doesn't it?'

'It sure does. How's your investigation going?' Fernanda asked, changing topics.

'Slowly. If he didn't have a heart attack, then it looks like the Senator was either strangled or poisoned. There are some marks on his neck, and there was a hole at the back of the toilet hut, so maybe someone could have put their hands in there and strangled him.'

'Jeez, that's terrible. And the poison?'

'He has burn marks inside his mouth as if he'd eaten something pretty caustic. Also, he had a terrible look on his face. If it's poison, then either one of the guests gave it to him somehow in full view of the others, which seems unlikely, or it was in his snacks or his meal.'

'The trail snacks are laid out every morning on a counter like a "pick-'n-mix", and guests can choose what they want. It would be hard to see how only Towers could be targeted and poisoned if it was in a snack.'

'Well, if it wasn't a snack he ate, then it would have to be either the soup Hugo served from his flask, or the meal from the canister Towers' lunch was in. However, more than one guest took the soup, so it was probably in the canister. Canisters that Hugo, the idiot, had rinsed out.'

'No, that's not possible either.'

'Why not?'

'Because Eduardo cooks all the picnic meals. He's this adorable little old man. He's been here since the hotel opened. Why would he poison an American senator? It doesn't make sense.'

'No, it doesn't, but first thing tomorrow I'm going to have to talk to this Eduardo.'

'If it wasn't him, then who was it? One of the guests? I've heard very mixed opinions about the Senator from our American guests. They seem to have either loved him or hated him.'

'Yes, I've talked to some of them, and the TripLux rep, too. Some Americans are funny travellers, don't you think? They're very tribal, always want to feel safe in their little group, protected in an American bubble, and the rich ones have such a sense of entitlement.'

'Come on, they're not all bad. I had a great time doing my masters at Berkeley. Californians are fun people. We have lots of lovely American guests from all over the States here, too.'

'Well, take the Senator and his pal, Dawson. Why come to a national park if you don't believe in them? Seems like they only came to get a selfie in front of various famous sights with their trophy wives to show to their friends back home.'

'That's unfair, too. Don't forget the whole national park movement was started in America. John Muir and all that! They had parks fifty years before Chile had its first. And then don't forget the Tompkins with their donations of land and their rewilding of other areas they own. They're heroes of mine.'

'Okay, okay, I take your point. They're great. I think that Dawson guy's got under my skin.'

'Doesn't pay to be a thin-skinned policeman in Chile these days.'

'No, it doesn't, and it doesn't pay to be a policeman who tells a civilian everything about his investigation either, so please keep what I've just told you confidential.'

'I will, I promise. But going back to the TripLux tourists, I do agree that doing all these sights in so many countries in so few days by private jet is weird. Do you know how much their trip is costing?'

'I have no idea.'

'Guess.'

'Okay. $20,000 a head.'

'Not even close,' said Fernanda, shaking her head. '$75,000 each.'

Nacho whistled and said, 'Wow! Why pay $75,000 to travel with a bunch of other people? For $75,000, I'd want to travel on my own and not put up with a crowd of people I might not like.'

'When I'm a multimillionaire and can afford a TripLux tour, I'll let you know,' said Fernanda, smiling and then yawning, in quick succession.

Just then Nacho's mobile phone rang. 'Shit, it's the DG,' he said, looking at the screen. 'I have to take this. I'm really sorry. I'll see you tomorrow. Thanks for the beer and all the help today. Bye.'

Nacho went into his own room next door and swiped to take the call.

'Good of you to answer, Hernández. I thought maybe you were sleeping on the job. What've you surmised so far?' grated the Director General's voice.

Nacho told the DG about the body and its recovery, the results of Dr Morgan's amateur autopsy, and that most of the Americans and the Brit on the hike all appeared to have a motive to kill Towers, varying from the weak to very strong. Nacho gave a potted history of the various hikers' experience with poisons, military training, and killing. He summarised that, although many had the motive, and there were two possible methods, the opportunity, in full view of the whole party, made it difficult to see how it was done. Nacho also told the DG about the roads being blocked.

'Splendid. The American Ambassador has been harassing our Foreign Ministry and I gather there's even been a president-to-president phone call demanding action. However, if this weather keeps up, preventing flights into the park, and the roads are blocked, then we have a good excuse to keep your American help at bay, not to mention those pesky journalists. I'll intervene and make sure the road clearance takes as long as possible even if the weather improves.'

'Thank you, sir. What's happening in the media? I haven't had time to look.'

'A lot of speculation, but since nobody knows anything other than the Senator is dead and that he might have died in "suspicious circumstances", they've not much to go on. The hotel guests down there with you have tweeted a few things about a police investigation which is adding fuel to the "suspicious death" fire, but again there's nothing substantive from them yet. Make sure you keep it that way.'

'Will do, sir. I've warned all the Senator's fellow hikers that they can't say anything about my investigation.'

'Right, I'll call again tomorrow. Goodnight, Hernández.'

'Goodnight, sir.'

Nacho hung up. He went back to the adjacent room, but as he put his head to the door, he could hear gentle snores coming from inside. Just as well, he thought, suddenly feeling very tired.

CHAPTER 12

Early the next morning, Nacho went down into the kitchen. An elderly chef in whites, with checked trousers and a toque on his head, was busy frying chicken and prawns, boiling a vast pan of rice, and heating a large vat of soup. Beside the chef was a line of vacuum canisters, ready to receive either chicken or prawn risotto, each with a tag for the guest's name and menu choice. Above him, pinned to a shelf, was a list of which guest hiking that day had requested which meal. Nacho had to admit the food smelled delicious. His stomach grumbled as he hadn't had breakfast yet.

'Eduardo? Hello, my name is Inspector Hernández, PDI. I have some questions for you,' said Nacho. As he advanced on the chef with his badge held out, he could see the man turn the colour of his jacket.

'What can I do for you, Señor? Would you like some of this for breakfast?'

'No, I have some questions for you. I presume you've heard about the important American who died the day before yesterday on a hike?'

The old man nodded, looking very uncomfortable, as if he knew what was coming next.

'Well, it looks like he may have been poisoned. That's one option for the cause of his death. If he was poisoned, then the food in one of these,' said Nacho pointing to the canisters, 'was the most likely source.'

The old man was visibly shaking now. Behind him came the smell of burning. Nacho leant past him and turned off the gas. As he did so, he noticed a chemical vermin trap on the floor under one of the kitchen's metal shelves. Nacho knew that mice were a real problem in Torres del Paine. Campers were always complaining about them, and the lodges and hotels had to keep on top of the pests too.

'Now, can you tell me how the poison may have got into a canister?' Nacho asked.

The old man shook his head and shrugged.

'You were cooking that morning, yes?'

This time the old man nodded his head.

'So, can you explain what happened?'

'No, Señor, I can't, but I can tell you this kitchen is clean. I am clean, too; I've never been in trouble in my life. I had nothing to do with this poor man's death, I swear on my mother's grave.'

The old man's plaintive little speech, along with his demeanor, almost convinced Nacho that he was telling the truth.

'So, after you fill these canisters, could someone interfere with them before the guests pick them up?'

'No, Señor. I take them up and serve them out in reception to the guests as they gather before their hikes. The hotel manager says it makes them feel a little bit special getting a gourmet picnic from a real chef.'

'Okay, carry on for now, but I may have more questions for you later. In the meantime, however, do you mind if I have a look around the kitchen and in your room?'

'No, Señor, I have nothing to hide. I am not responsible, I swear.'

A search of the kitchen and the chef's bedroom didn't turn up anything suspicious. The old man seemed to have nothing to hide, except maybe rat poison in plain sight.

Nacho went up to reception and talked to the concierge, Andrés Bravo. The man looked equally uncomfortable in Nacho's presence as their last interaction, and the concierge seemed relieved by the questions that were asked, and that none of them pertained to him.

'Did you see the guests picking up their lunch canisters the day before yesterday?'

'Yes, Señor.'

'Was there anything unusual about the process that day?'

'No, nothing serious, not really.'

'What do you mean by "nothing serious"?'

'It would be speculation and I don't want to get anyone into trouble.'

'And you know about getting into trouble, don't you, Bravo? Do your employers here know about your time inside? Armed robbery, wasn't it?'

'Please, sir, that was years ago. I was young and stupid. I've been clean since I got out, I swear.'

'Okay, so tell me what happened. It may not be significant to you, but it may help me.'

'Well, there was an argument between Eduardo, the chef who fills the lunch canisters, and the guest who died, Senator Towers. Mr Towers said he'd ordered chicken and Eduardo had given him prawns. The Senator called Eduardo all sorts of names, some of them a bit racist shall we say, and told him to change it. He humiliated Eduardo in front of the guests, me, the waiting guides, and the drivers. It wasn't possible to change of course, so another guest swapped with the Senator. Eduardo was nearly in tears afterwards. He showed me the order sheet, and sure enough Mr Towers had ticked prawns. It was his mistake and not Eduardo's.'

'Thank you, that's been most helpful. And don't worry, Bravo, your secret is safe with me.'

'Thank you, Señor. Glad to be of help. I'm sorry to say that this senator will not be missed by the staff here. He was quite abusive to many of us in the short time he was here. We've talked about it in the staff canteen.'

'Oh, what sort of things?'

'Well, being rude to the waiters. Then he had an argument the other day with Hugo, his guide, in addition to him shouting at Eduardo. It got quite heated.'

'What was it about? Do you know?'

'Hunting. The Senator was joined by Mr Dawson, who came to see him off. They were speculating that the park should be opened up to big game hunters to shoot some pumas. They said the llamas and deer would offer good game meat too. Seems like they didn't know guanacos are different from llamas. Anyway, Hugo gave them a lecture on the sanctity of the national park and they berated him, saying national parks were a waste of space, denying good hunting grounds, mineral exploitation, and so on. Eventually, Hugo walked away. I heard them laughing at him behind his back, calling him a tree-hugger, a llama-fucker, and other insults. I'm not sure if Hugo heard them. I hope not.'

'Thanks for that. Very interesting.'

Nacho thought about what he had just learned. If the Senator had been poisoned, but he'd eaten a lunch that wasn't designated for him in the first place, that meant the intended victim wasn't the politician after all if the poison had been in the canister. The intended victim would have been whoever had ordered his chicken meal in the first place.

Nacho went and had breakfast in the canteen and then sought out Eduardo once more. The chef was methodically cleaning his food preparation area.

'Hello again, Eduardo.'

'Señor?'

'I gather you and Senator Towers had a bit of an argument the other day? You failed to mention it.'

'It was nothing, Señor, just a mix-up in his order. He said a few unkind things, but you get guests like that occasionally. You have to take it and move on.'

'So, you didn't take the opportunity to add a little something to his canister after your row?'

'No, Señor, I didn't. Even if I'd thought about it – which I did not, I assure you – it would have been impossible. The guests were all milling around me, and anyway, the canisters are sealed with a plastic cable-tie so they don't open accidentally in a guest's rucksack.'

'Okay, and do you remember which guest swapped with Senator Towers?'

'Yes, Señor. It was Gabriel, Mr Thompson's companion.'

'But he wasn't on the hike.'

'No, Señor, but he came down to collect Mr Thompson's meal, and pick some snacks for his boss, who was apparently running a little late.'

Nacho thought that Gabriel's intervention was certainly one that Thompson himself would never have made, as he couldn't imagine the TV star swapping anything that would benefit the Senator. On the other hand, if Thompson had been the target of a poisoning, who would have wanted him dead? Alternatively, it seemed impossible that Gabriel could have slipped anything into the canister that Towers received as it was sealed by a cable-tie. He left the kitchen and went up to see if he could find Dr Morgan. She was sitting in the restaurant having breakfast with her husband.

'Sorry to bother you again, Doctor, but I need to ask you a couple of questions,' said Nacho, addressing the medical Morgan.

'Fire away,' she replied, brisk as always.

'Well, I wondered if it would be possible to poison a human with rat poison?'

'Rodenticide? Hmm, it's pretty unlikely. You see, most poisons put down for rats and mice are really anticoagulants. Have you heard of warfarin?'

'Yes, my father takes it.'

'Well, it's a blood thinner. Most rat poisons are a sort of diluted version of it. They cause the vermin to haemorrhage inside. Since warfarin is a drug that's fit for humans, you'd need a pretty significant dose to kill anyone. Anyway, if you think that's what did for Senator Towers, I'd suggest you think again. It wouldn't be quick, you'd need to use so much that any food used as camouflage would taste awful, and it wouldn't cause the ulceration we saw inside his mouth.'

'Right, thanks. And one more thing. The drugs used in chemically-induced abortions… could those be used to kill an adult?'

'No, sorry, again they're okay to use on adult humans since the expectant mother obviously survives. Third time lucky, maybe?'

'Maybe, but I'll have to come up with a third question first,' said Nacho, deflated that another two avenues to solving the Senator's death had been shut down. 'Enjoy your day, Dr Morgan. Oh, and you too, Dr Morgan number two.'

Nacho took a minute to look out of the picture window and enjoy the view. Across Lago Pehoé the Paine Massif was temporarily clear of cloud once more. The massif seemed like an alien sculpture. The sheer face of the massif rising from fifty metres to over 2,000 metres above sea level was one of the world's most abrupt changes in topography. While the massif was bathed in sunlight, its black-capped spires were stark against the sky, the pink of the granite walls were dazzling in the sunlight, the green of the unburned beech forests at the foot of the massif contrasted with the silver-grey of the fire-scorched area in the foreground, and the turquoise of the lake offered a different blue to the azure sky above. Nacho felt quite poetical as these thoughts passed through his mind.

'A peso for your thoughts?' asked a familiar voice.

Nacho turned and found Fernanda standing beside him. 'A peso? Haven't you heard? We've had rampant inflation. My thoughts are worth a million apiece.'

'Too expensive for me. You didn't come back last night after your phone call.'

'Actually, I did. But you were snoring by then.'

'I don't snore!' she said and hit him in the ribs with her elbow.

'Okay, I'm sorry. It must have been the dog.'

'I don't have a dog!' she said, hitting him again, but laughing this time. 'I thought that maybe we can have another beer tonight.'

'Maybe. I'll think about it,' said Nacho, trying hard to keep a straight face, as if her offer was one he would ever refuse.

'Don't think too hard. Your thoughts are expensive. Anyway, what have you been thinking?'

'I've been thinking I need to talk to Hugo again.'

'Okay, we can go and see him now. He only has a half-day walk today and it's in the afternoon. He'll be down in our office.'

'The hikes are still continuing after the Senator's death?'

'Some of the American guests don't seem bothered by it, as it's unclear why or how he died. Others, particularly the non-US citizens, feel they've paid a lot of money to come here, so they're going to enjoy it come what may. You know what they say in the theatre?'

'No, what do they say?'

'"The show must go on",' replied Fernanda. 'Anyway, given the winds, we're restricted by what we can do, so we're only out on the more sheltered hikes today and with fewer guests. I expect the spa will be busy instead of the trails.'

They went down into the hotel's basement and into the office set aside for the guides. It had a huge map of the national park on a wall with little flags on it depicting where the various hiking parties were. A whiteboard on another wall had the names of the guides, their designated hike for the day or half-day, and a list of their guests. A third wall held storage shelves stacked with rucksacks, walking poles, first aid kits, and other paraphernalia. The last wall had a chart showing the weather forecast at different scales for Chile, Patagonia and Torres del Paine. The forecast for the park warned of high winds. *Same old, same old*, thought Nacho.

Hugo was sitting at a table in the office reading a book. The table was cluttered with laptops, maps and notepads. There were two other guides sitting beside him. Fernanda asked them politely to leave and she and Nacho took the vacated chairs before Nacho started the interview.

'I have a few more questions for you, Hugo. You see, it looks like Senator Towers was poisoned, or possibly strangled. Most likely poisoned.'

'Okay,' said Hugo, still looking pretty shaken by the events.

'Let's go back to the hike up to the Valle del Francés. How did the Senator seem on the hike? Was he managing the terrain okay?'

'Yes, it didn't seem a problem for him, even that steep bit up to Mirador Sköttsberg. If anything, he was too keen. Like some of our guests, he seemed to think that as he'd paid his money he could do as he pleased, and he had to be reminded that I was to go in front. He actually seemed to want to show off how fit he was and that he was the leader. A sort of alpha-male thing. It would have been amusing if it hadn't been so irritating.'

'So, nothing untoward health-wise on the hike. And did he talk to many of the other guests?'

'Well, as I've said, the group was behind me and, as you know, the path is narrow, so, for most of it, we were in single file. I told you that he and Mr Ismail had a row. He got annoyed sometimes when guests stopped to take photographs, although he asked me to take a few of him on his phone with the view behind him. He was very specific that nobody should photo-bomb his pictures. Almost irrational about it, I'd say.'

'And when you stopped? What about then?'

'When we stopped, most of the other guests actually shunned him. He didn't seem too popular with his fellow Americans. The British and Australian guys talked to him a bit. But you know, it's so windy, and with hats or headbands on, it's difficult to hear, so there's never too much conversation anyway.'

'And then at Campamento Italiano, tell me again in detail what happened there.'

'Well, we crossed the bridge. That in itself was a problem, as more than one of them wanted to go at once, and they weren't willing to take turns for a couple of hikers coming the other way. Then we were up in the camp. I decided the weather was so bad that we'd eat in the wood rather than out on the moraine. So, I took them to an area on the edge of the campsite we've used before for picnics. There's a semicircle of large boulders to sit on off the grass, its upwind of the toilets, and the trees give a little shelter. Look, I told you all this yesterday,' said Hugo, sounding a bit exasperated.

'That's okay, tell me again,' ordered Nacho.

'I got the guests to sit down. I took off my pack and took out the blanket we use as a sort of tablecloth and spread it on the ground. I then laid out cutlery, my flasks, and so on. I gave them each a fork and invited them to take out their food canisters. Then I poured soup and passed it around, and most of them took a cup. I passed round the chilli-salt, and some of them added that, and I gave them bread, too. Then I got them all to hold up their cups as if they were giving a toast and took the photograph I showed you yesterday. We all started eating or sipping soup. I then passed around my penknife so they could snip the cable-ties on their hot food. Senator Towers got up in the middle of his lunch and rushed over to one of the chemical toilets.'

'Yesterday, you thought other guests went to the toilets, too?'

'Yes, Mr Thompson went. Or at least he went over there. I didn't see him go into one of the huts. On reflection, he may just have gone behind them, out of sight of the ladies in the party. Mr Ismail went over, too.'

'He didn't go into the Senator's toilet?'

'I don't know. I don't make a habit of studying what people do in toilets.'

'And then after a while you went to look for the Senator?'

'Yes, I was concerned he was gone a long time.'

'And you told me yesterday that you managed to unlock the door and found him already dead.'

'Yes, that's right.'

Nacho wondered if Hugo could have administered anything to a victim incapacitated by diarrhoea or food poisoning during their time alone.

'You see, Hugo, the problem I have is that the Senator was fine until the picnic and the only time he had any exclusive food was at that picnic. I can eliminate the trekking snacks, the soup, the bread, and the chilli-salt, as several people helped themselves to those, he had no exclusivity to them, and nothing happened to the others who took them. That leaves the meal in the canister or the period while you were alone with the Senator when you found him in the toilet. Now, I've checked, and Eduardo, the chef, seems an unlikely culprit, and the Senator was eating a meal originally assigned to Randy

Thompson. In addition, there's no evidence in Eduardo's room or the kitchen of anything suspicious, and the only poison he has access to wouldn't do a job on the Senator.'

'Well, I didn't do anything to him either!'

'No? Do you deny having an argument with the Senator and his friend, Dawson, on the morning of the hike?'

'No, I don't. But that was a difference of opinion. Before we set off on the hike, Senator Towers slapped me on the back and said something like "No hard feelings, son". I had never met the man before. Why would I kill him?'

'Why indeed? Okay, that's all for now.' Nacho got up to leave and then noticed the book Hugo had been reading. It was entitled *Examples of Geophagy from North America*. 'I see you're interested in geology. There's a university lecturer in geology who's one of the guests.'

'No, I'm not a geologist,' said Hugo, with a smile. 'This book is about geophagy. That's where animals deliberately eat clay or kaolin to counter stomach upsets. I'm studying for a PhD in zoopharmacognosy.'

'Zoo-what?'

'Zoopharmacognosy. That's when animals appear to self-medicate by eating clays with specific minerals in them, or plants which are medicinal. Many species seem to do it and there may be medicines that animals use that we humans can learn from. There are examples of sheep treating themselves for illnesses, for example. I'm studying whether the guanacos and huemuls here do the same. I gather data on them when I'm not leading hikes.'

'Ah, I see. Very interesting. Rather a niche area to get involved in?'

'My first degree was in chemistry and my masters was in pharmacology.'

'Pharmacology? Isn't that the study of the interaction between medicines – drugs that is – on humans and animals? Would that include the effect of poisons?'

'Whoa, wait a minute! Yes, I have some knowledge about such

things, but where would I get such substances here in Torres del Paine. You're barking up the wrong tree, Inspector. I had nothing to do with the death of the Senator. How many times do I have to tell you?'

'In that case you won't mind if I search your room?'

'No, go ahead, search where you like.'

Nacho left Hugo with Fernanda and went to search the guide's room in the staff accommodation block. After ten minutes of looking, he had found nothing. He went to his own room along the corridor to call the PDI Director General.

'Hello, sir, I'd like you to run some checks on the following individuals.'

Nacho gave the DG a list of names and the information he required, information not in the National Criminal Records files.

'In addition, sir, I'd like you to arrange a warrant, so I can search the rooms of the guests that were on the hike with the victim. I'm sure most wouldn't object if I asked, but from their reaction to my questioning, I'm sure some might take issue with me.'

'I've told you this is all low key, Hernández. I don't want to ask for a warrant, as I haven't asked for a prosecutor to be involved. We want the case solved, but we can't afford to annoy too many of these people. Sullivan, for instance, is a major investor in Chile and Ismail is talking about setting up his South American headquarters in Santiago. I'd never heard of her, but my daughter tells me this Ms Burroughs is quite a name on the Internet and, so far, she's been very positive towards Chile. I suggest you just get on with it.'

'Are you giving me an order, sir, to do a search without a warrant?'

'No, I'm not. I'm giving you an order to solve this case as soon as possible. Your career depends on it. Goodbye,' said the DG, and he terminated the call.

Nacho wasn't too pleased with the DG's instructions which were loud and clear, yet completely deniable on his boss's part. He wrestled in his mind with breaking approved procedures and conducting what would be illegal searches; searches that would be inadmissible in court if he found anything. Furthermore, he'd be exposing himself to an investigation by the PDI's internal affairs brigade if his actions got found out. In the end, Nacho's curiosity got the better of him, and he decided to go ahead and see what he could find in the guests' rooms, despite the career risk.

After crossing back over to the hotel, Nacho went to see the manager and got a pass keycard for the hotel by waving his badge and a search warrant at Gutiérrez. Nacho's bet paid off, and the manager didn't bother to read the warrant. If he had, Gutiérrez would have found out that it was a search warrant for a ferryman's address in Puerto Natales.

CHAPTER 13

Nacho checked in with reception to see which guests were where and learned that one or two were out on hikes, but the rest were at lunch. He put on a pair of latex gloves. Armed with his keycard he went to the first floor and, after knocking on the doors and getting no reply, he went through the first three rooms in quick succession. He found nothing of interest in the rooms of Taylor Burroughs or Hester Wilson. In Miranda Alexandra's, he found nothing of note except a small stash of marijuana, which he ignored. The next door opened when he knocked, and he found himself face to face with the new widow.

'Hello, Mrs Towers, I was just checking if you are all right,' lied Nacho.

'I'm fine. Have you found the sonofabitch who killed the old bastard yet?' she asked, slurring her words and swaying slightly, and Nacho could smell whisky on her breath. Over her shoulder he could see a selection of small bottles from the mini-bar, which confirmed his suspicions that she was enjoying a liquid lunch.

'No, Señora, I'm afraid I haven't yet, but I hope we'll soon clarify if it was natural causes or something sinister. I also hope that you'll be able to leave soon, probably tomorrow or the day after, with your husband's body. I'm sorry about the delay, but the weather has been unkind and the roads are blocked.'

'I should have been First Lady, you know, and now that shit has gone and spoiled it all. He's made a lot of enemies over the years, I can tell you. Always picking fights, always thinking he knew best, always having to show who was boss. Well, if it hadn't been for me bankrolling him all these years, he wouldn't have been a shoeshine boy, never mind a senator. All those years of putting up with his infidelities; the underage girls, the underhand deals. And do you know why I put up with all that? Do you? Do you, Mr Policeman?'

'No, I'm afraid I don't, Señora.'

'Because he promised to run for President and that I would be FLOTUS – First Lady! Just think of it all – The Miriam Towers Museum, The Miriam Towers College, The Miriam Towers High School, The *USS Miriam Towers*. And now the bastard's gone and gotten himself killed,' said the widow, and she started to cry.

'Again, I'm sorry for your loss, Mrs Towers, I really am.'

'*He* was no loss; First Lady was my loss. Old bastard,' she repeated.

'And do you have any idea who could have killed him, Señora, if it was murder?'

'Could have been anyone. My husband made friends and enemies with equal abandon. Some people loved him – mostly those who agreed with all the shit he said, or didn't have the brains to think for themselves. Or they hated him – because they disagreed with all the shit he said and had the brains to see past all his fake news and fact twisting.'

'I see,' said Nacho, wondering how to extricate himself from the conversation.

'Do you see? Are you sure, Mr Policeman? My husband would say anything, no matter how ridiculous, to keep his so-called base happy. He used to say in private that his job was to get re-elected, not represent the schmucks who voted for him. All his energy went into re-election, year after year. That's when he wasn't screwing some young porn star or beauty pageant winner. He was still at it, even in his seventies. Randy old goat.'

'So, no idea then?'

'I'd say that drag queen, Randy whatshisname. Either him or that creepie she-man of his. Also, the night Dwayne arrived here, I could hear that black guy ranting and raving at the hotel manager and that stupid TripLux gal that Dwayne wasn't meant to be on the tour and demanding a refund. And that Wilson woman, she hated him after what he did to her sister. And he did do it, Mr Policeman, he did do it. He confessed to me one night,' said Mrs Towers and then she suddenly pitched forward into Nacho and collapsed. He carried her into her room and laid her out on the super king-size bed. She was fast asleep, and Nacho tried to remember his first aid training and something about putting an unconscious person in the recovery position so they wouldn't choke if they vomited. He left her on her side, with her hands beside her head and her top leg bent, hoping his arrangement was correct, while fearing that the widow might slap him with a sexual assault suit for manhandling her body. Nacho hoped that she was so drunk that she wouldn't recall a conversation with him. He closed her door and continued his hunt for clues.

Nacho was conscious that the clock was ticking, so his room searches were necessarily perfunctory. In Callum Henderson's room, apart from the usual clothes and personal accessories, there were a lot of maps of the Falkland Islands, Argentina, and Patagonia, a DDL brochure of armed drones, a notebook of scribblings and sketches with "Operation Mikado" handwritten on its cover, a battered copy of a history book called *The Battle for the Falklands* by Max Hastings, and another book entitled *Executive Action* by Fabian Escalante. Intriguingly, the last was subtitled *638 Ways to Kill Fidel Castro*, and was about the CIA's attempts to assassinate the Cuban leader. There were several pages earmarked, including those relating to various poisoning devices. One paragraph highlighted by yellow marker was about using a hypodermic needle hidden in a fountain pen. In the photograph Hugo had taken, Henderson was sitting behind the Senator. *Could Henderson have stabbed Towers with a hypodermic and nobody noticed?* Nacho wondered.

He was then surprised to find a pistol in a zipped pocket in the ex-soldier's case. It was made of plastic, but neither looked like, or felt like, a toy. Being plastic, it was presumably undetectable by airport security. It appeared to be a single-shot weapon with a silencer attached. He wondered why the man needed a gun. It was illegal for foreigners to own weapons in Chile. Nacho slipped it into a large evidence bag and put it in his jacket pocket, planning to confront Henderson about it. Then he suddenly remembered learning about the Markov case in England during his police training. A Bulgarian defector was killed by secret agents firing a toxic ricin pellet from an umbrella sometime back in the late seventies. Nacho quickly eliminated his hypodermic theory and wondered if Henderson could have fired a poisonous pellet into the Senator using the silenced pistol. The pistol would have to be checked thoroughly by forensics.

His next port of call was Mo Ismail's room. Having just dismissed the hypodermic theory in favour of a poisoned pellet, Nacho had to re-evaluate as he found a box of syringes in Ismail's room. A set of small glass bottles were marked with "Regular Human Insulin", so he concluded that Ismail must be diabetic. Although the entrepreneur had convinced Nacho in his interview that he would have ruined Towers by hacking, if he'd chosen to do so, Nacho couldn't ignore his new find. *Was the mention of Wabayo poison in his interview a clever double bluff?* wondered Nacho. He went into the bathroom and beside the waste bin he found the small box with a slit on top labelled "sharps only" for disposing of razors, syringes, etc. that he'd noticed in the other rooms. He undid the catch and extracted the lining bag with its contents of two syringes with their short needles still attached, and put them in an evidence bag. If either of these had been used on Towers to inject poison, there would surely be traces the forensic lab scientists could detect.

In Jim Sullivan's room there were three photographs on a bedside table. One was a wedding photograph of Sullivan and his bride; the second was a female teenager standing in front of what Nacho knew was Uluru, the sacred rock in Australia's Red Centre and had "Love to Dad from Katy" scribbled in a corner; and the third was of three men beside an aeroplane. Nacho felt a pang of nostalgia as he realised the men were standing beside an English Electric Canberra. He'd had a model of the bomber when he'd been a child, proudly showing it to his friends as the Chilean Air Force had flown a few of the British-made jet. One of the men in the picture was clearly a younger Sullivan, and it was marked "With 2 Squadron at Phan Rang, 1969". He remembered that the Australian had served in the air force from his Wiki bio.

In Sullivan's en suite bathroom the only unusual thing he found was a small wooden chest with six tiny drawers in two rows. Its top was decorated with the outline of a lizard or crocodile made up of coloured dots. In the three drawers that he opened there were green, red, and yellow coloured powders in transparent plastic bags. On a small brass plaque on the front was inscribed the message, "Hope these help the pain, best wishes from the Elders of the Burraburra Tribe". He couldn't find anything of note in the Australian's luggage.

Nacho next searched Randy Thompson's room. In the suitcase of Gabriel, the American's partner, he found three tubes which obviously screwed together. At first, he couldn't figure out what they made. He was then shocked to find a quiver of darts and concluded the assembled tubes would form a blowgun. There was also a phial of liquid with a lurid skull and crossbones drawn on its label. Nacho's mind immediately went into overdrive. Like Henderson's pistol, a blowgun wouldn't be picked up by airport security scans, and if the liquid was in hold luggage, then it wouldn't need to be declared.

Did Thompson put the blowgun through the hole in Senator Towers' toilet cabin as he sat inside and blow a dart into the politician's neck, then stick a hand in to pull the dart out? Do I at last have the Holy Trinity for homicide detectives of motive, opportunity and method? wondered Nacho. He would have to check the Senator's body for puncture marks. He put the blowgun back as he found it, but took the phial and left the room.

Nacho abandoned his search and went down into the kitchen. It was quiet as the lunch service had just finished. Two kitchen porters who were washing up helped him lift the Senator's makeshift coffin out of the cold store. He told one of the men to go and see if Dr Morgan, the medical one, would come down and meet him.

While he was waiting, Nacho went on one of the house computers and typed "Wabayo" into Google. His hopes of a discovered perpetrator were dashed when he found out that the arrow poison was a thick brown pitch-like liquid. Neither of the syringes he'd recovered from Ismail's sharps' bin had any residue that matched that description. Through another search, Nacho found out that Ismail had funded a clinic for diabetics in Somalia, citing his own diabetes as the reason for this philanthropy, and thereby explaining the syringes and insulin in his effects.

'How can I help now?' asked Dr Morgan when she arrived. 'Found some more clues? This is all very exciting. I feel like I'm Dr Watson to your Sherlock Holmes.'

'Thank you for coming, Doctor. Yes, I may have found something and I need to check the body again. I believe there's a possibility that the Senator may have been poisoned through a dart fired from a blowgun, probably while he was sitting on the toilet. The hut he was in when he died had a hole at the rear, and maybe he could have been shot through that. Alternatively, he may have had a hypodermic needle stuck in his neck through the same hole. If that's the case then there should be a puncture mark on his neck as that would be the only exposed flesh on his back side. Because of the wind, I think he'd dressed in too many layers of clothing for a dart or needle to penetrate anywhere else on his body.'

'All right, let's have a look then, shall we?' said the doctor, slipping on latex gloves.

They unwrapped the clingfilm from the top of the Senator's chilled and stiff corpse.

'Well, at least freezing him has stopped the decay process. By now he'd have been a bloated, discoloured cadaver if you hadn't popped him in the freezer,' observed the doctor, 'and this would have been a much more disagreeable process, Inspector.'

They had a close look at the Senator's neck. There were no marks obvious to the naked eye. They checked his face, scalp and even inside his ears. After a few minutes, Nacho stood up, disappointed not to have found anything.

'So much for that theory, then,' said Dr Morgan.

'Let's try another one then. Could he have been shot in the back by a pellet from a handgun at short range. A gunshot could have penetrated the clothing layers and a pellet would explain why we found no bleeding wounds.'

With difficulty they turned the corpse over. They got quite excited by finding a rip in the back of the Senator's jacket. Nacho stuck a gloved finger into the hole.

'There's something hard in here,' he said and eventually he pulled out a small, spiked object. He looked at it and grimaced.

'What is it?' asked Dr Morgan.

'It's a calafate thorn.'

'Ah, yes, that berberis-like bush that one sees everywhere around here.'

'So much for my three options,' said Nacho, his voice heavy with disappointment.

'Yes, I'm afraid it looks unlikely that any of those were the modus operandi,' said Dr Morgan. 'But you know, I've been thinking. Firstly, the mouth ulcerations suggest to me that any poison was orally administered. And secondly, I believe those marks on his neck may have been self-inflicted. As the poison took hold with such a strong effect in his mouth, and presumably with his oesophagus burning too, he may have simply grabbed his own throat. You can see how strong his reaction to the poison was by the fact that after he did this his fists clenched tight. If he grabbed his throat with similar pressure, then the marks would have been from his own hands.'

'Right, thanks again, Doctor. So, I should really just focus on finding a poisoner, but a poisoner with a seemingly undetectable method of delivering the toxin,' said Nacho, shaking his head and screwing up his face, frustrated by his lack of progress after having had three possible leads dissolve in front of him.

'Yes, but what you really need is a full autopsy with our friend here opened up, poked about a bit, and with lots of lab tests on all his liquids and vital organs. Knowing the poison could help you understand how it was administered.'

By the time the Senator was rewrapped and boxed up again and back in his temporary morgue, it was late afternoon. Nacho felt he was going round in circles. Every time he thought he'd solved the Senator's death and figured out the perpetrator, his hopes were dashed. He needed more information and more evidence before he could accuse anyone of anything, while all the time he imagined the hot breath of the DG on the back of his neck.

Nacho was also bugged by the fact the crime couldn't have been premeditated as it wasn't known that Senator Towers was joining the TripLux party. Whoever killed him had used their proximity to him on the hike as an unexpected opportunity for murder and not a long-term pre-planned assassination. Yet none of the hikers seemed to have an obvious opportunity to administer poison to him. Although only Thompson had gone behind the Senator's toilet hut, it now looked like he hadn't strangled the Senator or used the blowgun from his partner's luggage. It also looked unlikely that Henderson had shot the Senator with his customised plastic pistol or that Ismail had stuck a needle in him.

Nacho kept coming back to Hugo and the window of opportunity created when the guide went to see if the Senator was okay. Hugo had studied pharmacology, so he could maybe have concocted some sort of poison. The two men had also had that altercation over national parks, but was that enough for one person to kill another?

His mind drifted back to the mysterious Henderson. While Nacho had found the firearm in Henderson's case, the Senator had clearly not been shot or had a pellet implanted in him. He replayed what Hugo had said up at the camp. The guide had said that Henderson had confirmed that the Senator was dead, and then helped carry the body out of the toilet. What if the Senator had merely fainted and Hugo had got it wrong? Then Henderson would have gone in to pick up the Senator and could have killed him then. The ex-special forces soldier would know how to kill with his bare hands so maybe the Senator hadn't been poisoned after all, just scalded his mouth with hot soup or too much chilli-salt. *How would I ever prove that?* wondered Nacho.

Just then his phone rang. It was the DG. Nacho rather liked the fact that he had the Director General of the PDI running errands for him. He went outside and found a sheltered spot out of the howling wind for his conversation.

CHAPTER 14

'Hernández, is that you?'

'Yes, sir.'

'Well, I've got that information you asked for on all those people. I got in touch with a senior contact of mine at FBI HQ in Washington. From what he said, there's nothing of any value regarding the three women involved, except Miranda Alexandra. You were right that there's been a lot of speculation about her poisoning her husbands, but the FBI say nothing was ever proven concerning her involvement in the deaths. They think that all those rumours about her killing animals near her father's drugstore were blown up by her publicists to create an air of mystery and menace around her to boost her early career. Apparently, before she became famous, she starred in a lot of horror B-movies and such publicity helped. Her PR team has only quashed them since she became a mainstream star.'

'Well, she certainly got pretty irate when I raised the topic, that's for sure.'

'Nothing on Mo Ismail either. He's always admitted to being a child soldier and that he had killed in the war in Somalia. However, he was cleared of any involvement in attacks on US troops there, like the raid on Mogadishu and so on. He's a practising Muslim, a non-drinker, and he has no felonies related to drugs or poisons, not even a drug bust for smoking joints as a student. He's diabetic, which is why he developed his first medical computer app after experiencing a hypoglycemic attack.'

'Okay, thanks, sir. I've more or less ruled him out as a suspect for now.'

'Nothing of interest on Randy Thompson either, but his partner, Gabriel, is another matter. Based on what the FBI said, I followed up with my opposite number in Brazil. Rio says this Gabriel is the son of an enforcer in the *favelas* for one of the local drug barons. Apparently, his father was nicknamed "The Silent Assassin" because he used a blowgun with darts tipped in curare poison to kill his victims. The father had been brought up in the Amazon rainforest before moving to Manaus and then on to Rio. There was an expectation that Gabriel would take over his father's trade before he was whisked away by Mr Thompson.'

'Now that's very interesting, sir, because I just found a blowgun in Gabriel's luggage today, along with what looks like a phial of poison.'

'Did he use it on the Senator, do you think?'

'Seems unlikely, sir. Gabriel wasn't on the hike with the Senator, so it would have had to be Randy Thompson who used it, and there was an opportunity to do so, I believe. However, there are no puncture wounds on any exposed area of the Senator that I could see when I re-examined the body with that British doctor I told you about. We may have missed something though, as we've no specialised equipment here, and could only see punctures visible to the naked eye.'

'Well, you need to talk to those two again. Importing such weapons into our country is illegal. Now on to the three non-US foreigners.'

'Did you say three, sir? There's only two, surely. Henderson and Sullivan.'

'There's three, as I will explain, Hernández, if you'll let me finish without interrupting all the time.'

'Yes, sir. Sorry, sir.' Nacho made a face at his phone and then panicked that he was on FaceTime and the DG would have seen him. He quickly checked his settings and then made a silent sigh of relief.

'I asked Interpol if there was anything on Henderson. Nothing to be found there. He seems like a bona fide businessman, even if he is an arms dealer of sorts. A contact at the British Embassy up here said Henderson was decorated in the Falklands War and that, before retiring from the Army, had been involved in several other clandestine operations in the Middle East. The attaché said that he couldn't, or wouldn't, tell me about them. Of all the people there with you, he is the trained assassin.'

'Look, sir, I'm sorry to interrupt, but Henderson had a pistol in his luggage. It's plastic and single shot. I think it may be one of those 3-D printed weapons. We've found 3-D printed gun parts being used in some of the crimes in Santiago, so such things are possible.'

'Well, again, that is illegal. You'll have to confront him too. The second non-US citizen is Mr Sullivan. Now, as you know, he is a major investor in Chile through his mines here. He's been quite a philanthropist too. Again, no criminal record of any sort. No evidence of bribery or corruption to get mining licences here in Chile or other countries, even in West Africa. His service record was with the Air Force. He was a bomber pilot with them in Vietnam and he was decorated by, not only his own government, but also the Americans and the South Vietnamese. So, while he may have been a killer in Vietnam, it was remotely and from a few thousand metres above the jungle. He's been knighted by the British Queen for his services to the Commonwealth and the environment.'

'I didn't know the Australians were in Vietnam.'

'No, neither did I, or if I did, I'd forgotten. Anyway, although he's low key, he's well thought of not only in Chile and Australia, but globally.'

Nacho remembered the photograph of the Canberra bomber with its inscription. He wondered if Phan Rang was in Vietnam.

'Now, finally we come to Hugo Sánchez, the guide from Colombia.'

'Colombia? That explains it! I couldn't place his accent and nobody told me he was Colombian. He never mentioned it. I just assumed he was Chilean.'

'Well, you were wrong, Hernández, weren't you? Hugo Sánchez isn't his real name. His real name is Hernando Valenciano. Seems like this Hugo is the nephew of a drug lord of one of the Colombian cartels. The story goes that he worked for the cartel as a chemist. However, Hugo wanted to apply his skills elsewhere and had a dream of becoming a legitimate academic. So, he escaped from his old life, bought a new identity, and came to Chile and enrolled in a PhD programme. To be even safer, he followed "The Road to the End of the World" and ended up, like you, in Patagonia.'

'How do we know all this, sir?'

'The PDI Intelligence Brigade are smarter than you and your colleagues think, Hernández.'

'Is there a warrant out for his arrest?'

'No, as far as we know he hasn't done anything wrong on Chilean soil and the Colombians have no direct proof to make a case to charge him and have him extradited.'

'He's admitted to me that he studied pharmacology, but says he specialises in something called zoopharmacognosy.'

'What the hell is that? Sounds like a dreadful disease.'

'It's where animals try to heal themselves when they're sick by eating different natural things like dirt and plants which have medicines in them. I must admit he seemed genuine enough about it. Very enthusiastic, in fact.'

'Well, it doesn't matter what it is because unfortunately for this Hugo, or whatever we call him, a pair of Colombians, tied to his old cartel, were seen recently in Punta Arenas, and so they may be on to him. I think you should find out if they've been in touch, and if he was ordered to kill Senator Towers.'

'Why would they want to kill Senator Towers, sir?'

'Because Senator Towers, in addition to having a role on their Armed Services Committee, was also involved with the Senate

Caucus on International Drug Control. Like all the subjects he talked about, his viewpoint was quite extreme, including using the US Air Force to bomb known drug cartel headquarters using these drones that have been so effective at taking out terrorists in the Middle East. There was recently an unexplained explosion at one of the cartel's warehouses, according to the FBI and my counterpart in Bogota. Since then, there's been much speculation in the Colombian criminal world that it had been an American drone strike. Maybe these drug lords wanted revenge and to send a message to the Senate Caucus. "Don't mess with us or we get personal", or something like that.'

'But that doesn't fit, sir. Few people knew that Towers was coming here after his fact-finding mission, so I doubt they could have ordered a hit at short notice, unless...' Nacho's voice trailed off.

'Unless what, Hernández?' demanded the DG, shouting down the phone. 'You've gone quiet on me.'

'Unless Hugo told them Towers was here, sir.'

'Exactly, Hernández. Now, I've given you some leads, so I suggest you get after them. And sort out these damned foreigners and their illegal weapons too.'

'Yes, sir. And when will the road be reopened?'

'The day after tomorrow. You still have thirty-six hours to find the assassin, so get on with it. The US media are getting a bit frantic. It seems that one of the Senator's friends down there with you has been making fun of the Chilean police. He's told some right-wing news channel via a phone interview that we haven't sent a real policeman to investigate, only some young "corn-chip detective". Shut him down, Hernández, shut him down.'

'Yes, sir, with pleasure.'

CHAPTER 15

After fighting his way through the wind, Nacho made it back into the hotel and passed through reception. By chance, Dawson was with the concierge, arguing about a request of his that hadn't been filled properly. A guide book on Chile, a wallet, and his smartphone lay beside Dawson on the concierge's desk. Bravo looked at Nacho and rolled his eyes, unseen by Dawson.

'Everything all right here, sir?' asked Nacho, distracting Dawson, and pocketing the man's phone.

'Yes, Corn Chip, I don't need your help sorting out this fellow here. Why don't you go and find out who killed Dwayne Towers instead of wasting my time? If you can, that is.'

Nacho walked off and crossed through the restaurant on his way to the guests' rooms. He dropped Dawson's phone into an ice bucket as he passed, hearing a satisfying swish as it sank below the water and ice mix. He saw Randy Thompson and his partner in the adjacent bar, having a laugh with Carlos. Nacho collared them and pulled them aside, and the three sat down in a booth.

'I've told you I'm not talking to you again without my attorney present,' said Thompson.

'Yes, I know, Señor. However, I was wondering if you could explain why there's a blowgun and a phial of liquid marked as if it was poison in the luggage in your room.'

'What the hell are you talking about, man? Have you been searching my room? Don't you need a warrant for that?'

'I believe it was in Gabriel's bag, Señor.'

Thompson turned and looked at his partner who in turn was staring at Nacho with a look of hatred written large on his face.

'Gabriel, is this true? What were you thinking about, for Christ's sake?'

'It was for self-defence. You know how people are always bugging you because of who you are, or what you are, or what you believe in. There are lots of crazies in the world. I brought it to protect you!' said Gabriel in a plaintive voice.

'Well, it's a good job we could find no puncture wounds from a dart on Senator Towers' body, Señors, or I'd have to arrest you two right now. However, I have taken the liberty of relieving you of the phial of liquid and it will have to be tested in a forensic lab when we can get out of here. It will be compared to any evidence gleaned from Senator Towers' remains after his autopsy. If the contents of this phial match the poison that killed Towers, then you will be arrested. Also, I have to tell you, that until that analysis is complete, you will not be allowed to leave Chile. That's all for now, Señors.'

As he left the bar, Dawson stopped him with a shout, 'Hey, Corn Chip, someone's stolen my phone!'

'I'm sorry, sir, I'm far too busy trying to find out how Senator Towers died to be bothered with petty crime. Call the Carabineros in Puerto Natales,' replied Nacho, trying to ensure that he didn't sound too self-satisfied, before moving off.

Nacho couldn't find Callum Henderson in any of the public rooms so he assumed the ex-soldier was in his bedroom. Mindful that he was visiting a trained assassin, Nacho went to his own room and retrieved his service pistol before going up to knock on Henderson's door.

As the door swung back, Nacho entered the room with his pistol in his hand. He was suddenly grabbed from behind the door, had his weapon twisted from him, flung on his back, winded, and left staring up at Henderson. The ex-soldier was holding Nacho's pistol in an arm's length two-handed grip with the barrel pointed directly at Nacho's head.

'Inspector Hernández? Well, you're a lucky boy. It doesn't pay to enter an SAS man's room with a pistol. You're lucky I didn't give you a double tap. Here, let me help you up.'

Henderson helped Nacho to his feet and handed him his pistol, butt first.

'Sorry about that. Force of habit. Training, you see. I wasn't intending to assault a police officer as I didn't know who you were. Just saw the gun. Nothing personal, Inspector.'

'What's a double tap?' asked Nacho, wheezing while holding his back.

'Two shots in quick succession to the same spot. A technique used by special forces. I'm sure your own Lautaro commandos will use it.'

'Sorry, Señor, you're right. I shouldn't have come in with a drawn weapon.' Nacho now realised that if he'd had to fight Henderson it would not have been a fair bout, and he was actually relieved by the man's seemingly relaxed attitude.

'I've come to talk to you about this,' said Nacho taking out the plastic pistol from his pocket.

'Ah, so you searched my room while I was out and you found my little toy.'

'Am I correct in saying it's a plastic 3-D printed pistol? Plastic, but still lethal.'

'Yes, very good, Inspector.'

'And why do you have that, Señor?'

'Again, force of habit. Just like tackling you a few minutes ago. Once an SAS Trooper, always an SAS Trooper. I just felt that being a Falklands veteran in this part of the world, and visiting the various sites I'd been at back in '82, particularly when I visit the Argentinian side as I plan to do next, that, well, you know, old animosities die hard. I was a bit worried some old Argie combatant from back then might take exception to me. We won and we killed a lot of their soldiers. And sailors. And airmen for that matter. That's why.'

'I've had to confiscate it, Señor. It is illegal for foreigners to own weapons in Chile.'

'Of course, now I've been found out. I'm sure I'll be able to find somewhere to print another one, Inspector.'

'Why the silencer?'

'Again, force of habit,' said Henderson with a shrug.

Nacho wasn't sure he believed him. 'And single shot? No double tap, then?'

'The only weapon you have, is the best weapon you have, Inspector.'

'Well, it's better you have no weapon for the rest of your stay in Chile, Señor.'

'If you say so. Now, anything else I can do for you, Inspector?'

'Yes, there is. You were the one who pulled Senator Towers out of the toilet, weren't you?'

'Yes, that's right.'

'And how long did that take? You see, I reckon that as you did that, you'd have had to have your back to the other hikers and so they couldn't have seen what you were up to with him.'

'Are you suggesting I molested a dead man when his pants were down?' asked Henderson, with a grin. 'I can assure you I'm not a gay necrophiliac, Inspector.'

'No, Señor, I'm suggesting you had the opportunity to administer a poison to Senator Towers who might not actually have been dead at that point.'

'Ah, I see. It's a fair cop, guv. I went and stabbed him with my fountain pen containing the cyanide capsule.'

'You what?' asked Nacho, astonished at Henderson's sudden confession.

Henderson laughed and said, 'I'm not bloody James Bond, you know. I don't have a lot of Secret Squirrel gadgets given to me by Q.'

'But in a book you're reading, that's exactly how the CIA planned to assassinate Fidel Castro.'

'Ah, so you found that too? That's just research for a book I'm planning to write. Books by ex-SAS men seem to sell well. You know the sort of stuff, Andy McNab, Chris Ryan and so on.'

'Sorry, I've never heard of them,' said Nacho, shaking his head.

'Really? They're good action stuff. Anyway, I'm afraid, Inspector, that rather crude, little pistol is the full extent of my armoury, other than my bare hands of course. So, no, Inspector, I did not administer any poison to Senator Towers. He was as dead as a dodo when I got to him. As I think I said to you before, I've seen a lot of dead men in my old line of work and he was definitely as dead as Monty Python's parrot.'

The rapid-fire mix of British cultural references confused Nacho somewhat, but he got the drift of Henderson's denial. The casual attitude to death was presumably that of an ex-soldier. He'd heard that many men suffered from post-traumatic stress disorder after being in combat, but unless it was all an act, Henderson didn't seem to be one of those unfortunates.

'Anything else, Inspector?' Henderson repeated.

'No, that will do for now, Mr Henderson. However, until I resolve how Senator Towers died, I'm afraid you will not be allowed to leave the country.'

'Understood and understandable. I hope you have a pleasant evening, Inspector, and again, sorry for the rough and tumble. No hard feelings?'

'Only in my back, Señor,' said Nacho with a grimace as he left Henderson's room.

Nacho went down to the guides' area and found Hugo, fresh back from the afternoon hike. They went to Hugo's room.

'I fear, Hugo, that you've been less than honest with me.'

'No, Inspector, I have not. I did not kill Senator Towers, I swear.'

'Well, you could have told me that you were actually a Colombian called Hernando Valenciano. You could also have told me that you used to work for a cartel and that your uncle was a drug lord. And, you could have told me that you worked for him as a chemist and are therefore a bit more experienced with drugs than you let on.'

Hugo looked crestfallen, and blurted, 'How did you find out?'

'The police in our two countries talk, and we have an intelligence unit.'

'I never hid from you that I had studied pharmacology and you never asked where I was from.'

'Well, our intelligence unit has also been communicating with the FBI and it seems that they fear your old cartel may have put out a contract on Senator Towers. And it seems to me that you've fulfilled the contract by using your chemist's skills to poison him when on the hike.' Nacho knew he was stretching here, but he wanted to see what Hugo would say.

'I know nothing about that, nothing,' said Hugo, his high voice displaying his anxiety.

'Do you deny that on your last days off on rotation you went to Punta Arenas and that you were met there by two men from your uncle's cartel?' asked Nacho, guessing now.

'How did you know that?' whispered Hugo.

'Again, intelligence,' said Nacho, thinking *mine, though, rather than Santiago's*. 'What did you talk about?'

'We didn't talk about Senator Towers, believe me, Inspector. When I was last in Punta Arenas it hadn't been announced that the Senator would be joining the TripLux party up here. They couldn't have known that either. That's not what they wanted.'

'All right, you've admitted you met them and talked, so, what was it they wanted?'

'I can't tell you, Inspector. They'll come looking for and kill me if I tell you anything,' said Hugo, appearing to Nacho to be genuinely terrified.

'Hugo, if you don't tell me, I am going to arrest you right now and charge you with the murder of Senator Dwayne Towers,' said Nacho, hoping that Hugo didn't know that in Chile this would have been impossible without a prosecutor's order. Hugo was as white as a sheet by now, so Nacho pressed his advantage. 'You can look forward to a long stretch in prison here in Chile, or worse, you could be extradited to the US where they still have the death penalty for certain crimes. I'm sure assassinating a senator would fall into that category.'

'Okay, I'll tell you, but you have to protect me.'

'If you're not guilty of killing the Senator, then I can have you enrolled in our witness protection scheme.'

'All right. It's true the guys from the cartel spoke to me. But it wasn't about Senator Towers. After their warehouse was bombed, they wanted to make a statement against the US and send a warning that they, too, have a long reach. They'd monitored various TripLux tours, knowing the company specialised in high-worth individuals of mostly US citizenship. They had learned somehow that I was down here and they also knew that a TripLux party was coming. They told me I'd be eliminated if I didn't help them.'

'So, what did they ask you to do?'

'They plan to hold up and rob the TripLux party on its way back to pick up their private jet in Punta Arenas. Superficially, it will look like it's been done by dissident Chileans, protesting against wealthy people. But they'll send a message back to Washington somehow, so that the CIA and FBI will know it was the cartel and not to mess with them. This time it's just a robbery that's planned, but if the US strikes at them again, it could be hostages, or even a mass murder. It's going to be a warning shot. I've to call them and tell them when the Americans leave.'

'Right, I'll have to let my HQ know that you've confessed to this plot. I'll see that you're protected. In the meantime, don't run. The road east is blocked by a landslide, but in case you fancy your chances over there, I plan to let the border guards at Cerro Castillo know about you, so that you can't escape into Argentina. The road south won't be open until tomorrow. So, for now you're stuck. I won't formally arrest you and imprison you. If that got out around here, it's sure to leak to the press via social media from one of the guests. I don't want to draw attention to you in case any of this gets back to your uncle's men. I'd rather we took them by surprise.'

'Thank you, Inspector. I'm really grateful,' said Hugo, sighing with relief.

'One other thing, Hugo, as a favour to me for helping you escape these gangsters, do you know anything about curare from your studies?'

'Sure. It's used as a plant-based poison in the Amazon basin by the indigenous peoples. They dip the darts of their blowguns in it, and then fire them at their prey when hunting.'

'What does it do to the prey?'

'In some cases, it stuns the animals, in others it kills them.'

'How does it work?'

'It causes paralysis and eventually asphyxiation by shutting down the diaphragm.'

Nacho was mindful that he'd found no puncture marks on Towers, but now wondered if Thompson had put his hand in through the hole behind the sitting politician, grabbed the Senator's neck and emptied curare down the man's throat. He took the phial of liquid he'd found in Gabriel's luggage out and showed it to Hugo. The phial wasn't completely full.

'What would happen if, instead of using a blowgun and dart, you put the small amount of curare missing from this phial down someone's throat?' Nacho asked Hugo.

'Not much, I suspect.'

'But you just said it was a poison!' said Nacho, exasperated.

'Yes, it's toxic when injected into the bloodstream, but not the gastrointestinal system. It's harmless if taken orally. Its compounds are too large to pass through the gut into the blood where it causes the damage. That's why it's safe to eat prey killed by curare.'

Damn, thought Nacho, *another theory blown up in smoke and another suspect off the hook.* 'Thanks anyway, Hugo,' he said and turned to leave.

'No worries. It would be different if it was frogs.'

Nacho turned around and said, 'Frogs? What do you mean, frogs?'

'Poison frogs.'

'Poison frogs?' asked Nacho, thinking he was beginning to sound like a demented parrot.

'Yes. If the liquid you have there is usually for a blowdart and it isn't curare, then it may be from a poison frog. The natives in some parts of the rainforest gather secretions from glands under the skin of poison frogs and use them to kill. The poisons in the secretions are highly toxic – and I mean highly toxic – so be careful with that stuff.'

'I didn't know frogs hunted prey that way,' said Nacho, surprised, thinking of David Attenborough documentaries where frogs shot out their tongues to catch passing dozy flies.

'They don't. It's purely a defence mechanism. They're brightly coloured to warn off predators, but if that fails, then the frogs poison anything that catches them and tries to eat them. That's why it's their skin that's so dangerous.'

Nacho thought how appropriate this would be for Thompson to use this as a method for killing Senator Towers. In his "American Queen" guise, he was brightly coloured, but with his Marine training he was deadly. His whole surprise about Gabriel's phial could just have been an act.

'Right, thanks again, Hugo,' said Nacho, and he left for his own room.

Once there, he called the DG. He told him about the cartel's plan and the DG agreed to take steps to prevent the planned hijacking and robbery.

'By the way, Hernández,' said the DG, 'it's still too windy to use cranes to shift that cattle train blocking the bridge or for helicopters to land in the park. However, a bulldozer is on its way to push the trailers aside. I reckon you've only got until noon tomorrow before you'll be pulled from the case and we'll have to let our American friends take over. That would hurt my pride and that of all of the PDI. Solve it!'

No pressure there then, thought Nacho after the call. He pulled out the photograph of the lunch party once more, looking for inspiration. Which one of the guests had killed Towers if it wasn't Hugo? Was it Thompson after all? Something caught his attention. A detail he hadn't noticed before. He went back to Hugo's room.

'What is it this time?' asked Hugo, with a sigh.

'When you took the photograph, you said the other day that it was before you passed round your penknife to cut the cable-ties on the food canisters, yes?'

'I think so.'

'That's not good enough. Is it correct?'

Hugo thought for a while before speaking. He was obviously replaying the scene at the Campamento Italiano again in his head. 'Yes, that's right. I poured the soup first and then people can either drink it on its own or with the hot rice and chicken or prawns.'

'Okay, thanks.'

Nacho left a bewildered Hugo, and battled the wind back to the main hotel building. He went directly up to Randy Thompson's room and hammered on the door.

'What the hell do you want now?' asked an angry Thompson when he opened the door and saw who it was. 'This is verging on harassment, Inspector. Have you got something against gays? Are you one of these anti-LGBT freaks?'

'No, Señor, I am not harassing you, but the death of a US senator is a serious matter. I'm afraid I have more questions for you, or rather Gabriel. May I come in?'

'I suppose so, but make it quick.'

Nacho entered the room to find both men in their hotel towelling robes, obviously getting ready for bed.

'Now, Gabriel, I believe you swapped lunches with Senator Towers the other day after there was a mix-up in the allocation of food canisters?'

'That's right.'

'Why did you do that?'

'I felt sorry for the old chef. Towers was treating him like a piece of shit. I've been treated the same way in my time, so I rescued him. I know Randy doesn't mind if he eats prawns or chicken, so it was no big deal.'

'And what did you do to the canister as you swapped them?'

'What do you mean?'

'Did you add any of this to the Senator's new canister before you handed it over?' asked Nacho taking Gabriel's phial out of his pocket.

'No, I didn't.'

'I have photographic proof that the Senator's canister was tampered with. You see the canisters are sealed with a cable-tie and in the photograph all the other guests' canisters are still sealed, but Towers' isn't.'

'Maybe he opened it himself before the others?' asked Thompson.

'Did you see him do that?'

'No, I was sitting behind him.'

'And we didn't find a penknife in his pockets. No, I think Gabriel here opened it down in the foyer before he swapped the canisters over and added some of this poison to the Senator's food. I believe this is poison frog toxin, and I've talked to a pharmacologist and he says it's deadly.'

'No, that's not true,' said Gabriel. Nacho stared hard at the Brazilian, and eventually Gabriel spoke again. 'Okay, okay, I did open the canister, but I didn't add any of that stuff to it.'

'Why did you open it?'

'I knew the Senator hated Randy and said a lot of bad stuff about him. About me, too. So, I opened it and I spat into it.'

'You spat into it?' asked Nacho, disgusted. For some reason this seemed worse than adding poison.

'Yes, I wanted to add a little HIV-positive saliva to the Senator's lunch. He was a horrible man.'

Thompson laughed at the explanation and reached out and ruffled Gabriel's hair.

'You're HIV-positive?' asked Nacho.

'Yeah,' said Gabriel, now looking defiantly back at Nacho.

'I'm sorry to hear that,' said Nacho, thinking he'd better check the truth of this.

'And it's not poison frog toxin in the phial. It is curare. A mild mix. That's what your analysis will show, I promise.'

'If what you say is true, then you'll be in the clear. However, it will be the autopsy that will reveal if the liquid in this phial killed Towers or not. If it didn't, then you'll be free to go, but in the meantime, you're still blocked from leaving the country. That's all for now.'

Nacho felt he needed to take his mind off the case for a while. He sought out Fernanda in the staff canteen and afterwards they retired to her room for a beer. After a few drinks, one thing led to another.

CHAPTER 16

'Wow, that was fantastic. I'm flattered. I thought I'd be too young for you based on your reputation,' said a naked Fernanda, flopping back on the pillows, a broad smile on her face.

'What do you mean my reputation?' asked Nacho, curious.

'When I took over from you at the Explora, the other guides used to laugh that the lady guests would miss you. You had a reputation that you only liked women of a certain age. Over forty, shall we say?'

'Ah, I see. I wasn't some sort of gigolo, you know. It was just that at times some of those ladies needed comforting when they were lonely. And, anyway, those grateful ladies helped pay for my college education. Also, those same ladies taught me a few things too, and you've just benefited from that experience,' said Nacho, laughing.

'I certainly did, but I really didn't think you were some sort of a gigolo, honestly.'

'I never propositioned them. They came on to me and then gave me presents afterwards. That's all. It would have been rude to refuse their gifts. Well, that's my story, officer, and I'm sticking to it.'

They were both giggling when Fernanda's smartphone rang.

'Who could this be at this time of night?' asked Fernanda. 'I'd better answer it. It's a Santiago number. I hope nothing has happened to my uncle.'

She swiped and Nacho suddenly heard a familiar voice on the line, despite the phone not being on speaker mode.

'Yes, yes, I'll find him and get him to call you on this number. Yes, I understand, he has to use this phone to call you. All right, I'll go and waken him,' said Fernanda, and she finished the call.

'That was some guy looking for you. He said his initials were DG and you'd know who it was. I've to find you and get you to call him on the number he just used, but from my phone. You've not to use yours. He was very insistent on that.'

Nacho took her phone and called the DG back. 'Hello, sir?'

'Hernández, I'm glad that young lady tracked you down so quickly.'

'Why did you call her, sir, and why are we not using our own phones?'

'I called her because the hotel's website says she's the Head Guide and then I got our IT guys to find her number. Who better to find you than a guide? Though she seemed to find you very quickly, no?'

'Our rooms are right next to each other, sir,' replied Nacho, pleased that he hadn't actually told the DG a lie, just made a true statement. He put his finger to his lips to ensure Fernanda's silence as she suppressed a giggle.

'Well, anyway, we're not using our own phones because the whole situation regarding Senator Towers has escalated. Since a US senior politician has been killed on Chilean territory and it may affect Chile's relationship with the US, our Intelligence Service, ANI, has got in on the act. They're claiming this has now become a national security issue. I believe they'll be listening in on our normal phones, even if that's against the rules. They're sending one of their men down, a Captain Figueroa, and he's a mean bastard I'm told. A relic from the Pinochet era who has somehow survived until now. The Americans have sent some FBI G-men with him. You need a result, but if you don't get it, be very wary of Figueroa. I'm just calling to warn you.'

'Right, thank you, sir.'

'And the Prosecutor's Office has got wind of this investigation too, but don't worry I'll deal with them.'

'Thanks again, sir.'

'Okay, I'll leave you to get on with whatever it was you were doing.'

Nacho swiped Fernanda's phone to terminate the call.

'What was all that about?' asked Fernanda.

'It was my big boss just calling to warn me that I'm running out of time.'

'Well, I hope you've got time to stay a little longer.'

'Oh, I think I'll manage. Now, where were we?'

*

Early the next morning as Nacho and Fernanda lay asleep, intertwined in her bed, they were rudely awakened by banging on her door.

'Fernanda, Fernanda, come quickly! Something awful has happened. Esmerelda is dead. She's been killed,' yelled an anguished female voice from the corridor.

'I'll be right there!' Fernanda shouted back.

'Okay, I'll see you at the salt lick.'

'I think that was Paulina, one of the guides. She was Esmerelda's friend,' said Fernanda, leaping out of bed and dressing.

'Who the hell is Esmerelda?' asked Nacho, concerned that he had a second murder to deal with.

'She's the hotel's pet huemul deer.'

'What?'

'She's a deer that got separated from her herd and has been living around the hotel for a few months. She had been hit by a car in the park and had developed a bit of a limp. The guides clubbed together to pay for a vet to come up and look at her. She's okay now, but has seemed reluctant to leave us. We don't feed her or anything, but we just look out for her. We haven't seen her for a couple of days and then she was seen last night in the area. She often wanders off and then comes back.'

Nacho also got dressed and they went out and round the back of the guides' accommodation block. The sun was barely over the horizon and it was bitterly cold, the wind chill, as ever in Torres del Paine, lowering the temperature by several degrees. In the half-light they could see a human figure standing over a fallen animal. As they got closer, Nacho could see a huemul lying on the ground. The deer had a shaggy brown coat with a white underside and would have been about a metre tall when standing. Its head had large, pointed ears and bore no antlers, so Nacho knew that it was a female. The deer's lips were pulled back in some sort of death throes rictus. He knelt down beside it and touched the animal. It was still warm.

'I didn't know there were salt licks in the park,' Nacho said to the two guides.

'It's not a naturally occurring lick. It's Hugo's. It's one of his experiments for his PhD. He always empties his salt pot over there against that stone. You know, the chilli-salt we use for the lunchtime soup for the guests? It gives it a bit of a kick,' explained Fernanda.

'And then he photographs the animals using that camera up there,' added Paulina, pointing to a box on a pole where Nacho could just make out a lens poking out of a hole. 'It's got a motion sensor below it. Anything that comes to the lick gets photographed. Esmerelda is, or rather was, a frequent early-morning visitor. Poor Esmerelda.' Paulina began to cry, and Fernanda put her arm around her.

'Shit,' said Nacho, louder than he meant to. 'I need to go and talk to Hugo again. Sonofabitch just ingratiated himself with me to help him escape his troubles, when all along he was the killer!'

'I'll come with you,' said Fernanda and they set off back to the guides' accommodation.

'What's the matter? Why are you so angry?' asked Fernanda as Nacho banged on Hugo's bedroom door. When the guide opened it, he was dressed in a yellow T-shirt and boxers.

'What's wrong? What am I supposed to have done now?' asked Hugo, a bit groggy from sleep.

'Esmerelda's been found dead at your salt lick,' replied Fernanda.

'My salt lick? But how?'

'We don't know yet, for sure. Why do you have a salt lick anyway?' asked Nacho.

'It's part of my research. As I explained before, in zoopharmacognosy we think that animals eat certain plants or soil if they're sick and that these act as medicine. However, it may also be that they eat specific plants or add minerals to their diets, in the same way as humans do with vitamin pills to stay healthy. Some of the vitamins may come from salt licks. Most salt isn't pure sodium chloride, you see, but it acts in a way that concentrates other minerals which animals may need. These act as a prophylactic, or preventative, if you will.'

'And the deer eat chilli-salt?' asked Nacho, sceptical about Hugo's story.

'The deer primarily eat lenga trees and bushes. That's their preferred diet, but they also eat the tussock grass and other tough plants too. Their tongues can handle chilli, believe me.'

'And that gives you a great cover story for how you killed Senator Towers. You poisoned him with a dose of chilli-salt in his lunchtime soup, didn't you?'

'What are you talking about?'

'Do you deny emptying your salt cellar after the hike onto the stone you've used to create a salt lick?'

'No, I don't. I can't. And, anyway, my camera beside it is triggered by motion so it always takes a picture of me when I do it.'

'How better to dispose of the evidence than to throw it away in plain sight.'

'But you're missing something, surely?'

'What am I missing?' asked Nacho, angry with himself as well as Hugo, for letting the guide divert him with his Columbian gangster story and his advice on poisons.

'Several other guests used the chilli-salt before it got passed round to Senator Towers.'

'So, you're claiming you never gave it to him directly, but it got passed from guest to guest?'

'Yes, exactly, and the other guests who had the salt mix are all okay. I'm sure if you ask them, they'll confirm that's how it was.'

Nacho was now even angrier with himself after Hugo had pointed out this obvious flaw in his latest theory. However, he ploughed on.

'Do you have your salt pot here? The cellar you used on the hike?'

'Yes, it's still in my rucksack, I think.'

'I'll need to keep it, please, for forensic analysis to compare its contents to what killed the Senator once we get his autopsy done.'

Hugo passed over a large glass salt pot with a silver perforated screw top. Nacho held it up to sniff at it to see if he could detect any untoward chemicals.

'Wait a minute, that's not my salt pot,' exclaimed Hugo pointing at the cellar's base.

'What do you mean?'

'Look, the number on the bottom, it's a seven.'

'So?' asked Nacho, turning the salt pot over and noting a number 7 marked on the bottom in thick felt pen.

'I always take the salt cellar with the number 10 on it. That's my lucky number. I was born on 10 October. 10/10, see? And look,' said Hugo turning around and pointing over his shoulder to the back of his shirt.

Nacho now realised it wasn't just a yellow T-shirt Hugo had on, but a Colombian national football team strip. On the back, above a large number 10, was the name "Valderrama", a famous Colombian forward from the nineties.

'Then whose salt pot is number 7 and why do they have numbers anyway?'

'It's to allow Eduardo to keep track in case any guests have a special request and want to use a salt substitute,' explained Fernanda. 'Some of the guests worry about their blood pressure and salt's not good for that. Too much raises the pressure. The guests notify him as picnic chef in their menu request. Then it's easier for him and the guides to just change the whole pot out. Usually he uses a mix of Atacama pink salt and either goat's horn chillies or his special *merkén* mix. However, he has some low sodium substitutes he can replace the salt with if requested.'

'Okay, I understand that,' said Nacho, 'but does anyone specifically take number 7?'

'Miguel takes number 7 usually. He's a massive fan of my namesake, your Alexis Sánchez, the Chile number 7,' answered Hugo.

'It's true,' confirmed Fernanda. 'The boys are always squabbling about silly things like that. Girls would never get so upset about some salt and red powder.'

'Red powder,' echoed Nacho. He turned to Fernanda and asked, 'Do you keep a record of which guests go on each hike or do you just junk the lists after it's over?'

'No, we keep a record, or at least reception does. Why, what's the matter?'

'You've just given me an idea. I need to check something first.'

Nacho left the two others and raced over to the hotel reception. The desk clerk brought up on his computer screen the guest list of the hike that Miguel had led on the day before the Senator was killed. There was one name common to both Miguel's hike and the one Hugo had led the day after.

'What time did Miguel's hike leave on this day?' he asked the clerk, pointing at the screen.

'That's the Alto del Toro hike. It usually leaves about 10 am.'

'And what time did Senator Towers arrive here?'

'He arrived quite early as I recall. Let me look at his check-in time.'

The clerk's fingers danced across his keyboard before he said, 'Yes, I was right, he checked in about 9.30 am.'

'Really? He must have set off early from Punta Arenas Airport or a hotel to get here by then.'

'Oh, no. He came by helicopter. His was the last flight in before the wind really picked up. He was flown in by the Air Force from the Puerto Montt base.'

'And where do the hiking groups meet before their departure?'

'Over there. They collect their snacks, lunches, and drinks from Eduardo at that counter and then look at the map on the wall there, get a briefing from their guide, and then go out to get their van or go down to the pier.'

Nacho noted that the hike departure area had a clear view of anyone checking in.

'And when did Senator Towers book his hike for the next day?'

'He did it directly after he registered. I remember it well. He said he needed to stretch his legs and get some good photographs of himself out in the wilds. He made some joke about going barechested like President Putin to show his voters how healthy he was.'

'Thanks, you've been a great help,' Nacho told the clerk.

As he was departing the desk, he heard a voice calling him. It was Howie Dawson, the late Senator's friend.

'Hey, Corn Chip, you found out anything more about Dwayne?'

'As I told you the other night, inquiries are proceeding, Mr Dawson.'

'Sounds like you need the FBI to come down here and help you amateurs out.'

'That won't be necessary, Mr Dawson(*ofabitch*),' replied Nacho, the last bit said quietly to himself.

Nacho went across to his room in the guides' accommodation and logged on to his laptop. A number of small throwaway phrases said by people over the last couple of days were running in his mind. An idea had crystallised in his brain, and he now thought he understood the method and opportunity for the Senator's murder, but not the motive. He brought up the picture of the Senator's last lunch that Hugo had sent to him and looked at it closely. Then he entered a string of search queries in Google. He was surprised that the source that answered one of his questions wasn't from the country he expected. His mobile phone rang as he closed his laptop down. It was Fernanda.

'That DG guy phoned again,' she told him. 'He said to tell you the roadblock has been cleared and the bridge is being inspected. He also said your expected visitors should be with you in a couple of hours. Who are you expecting?'

'I'll explain later, Fernanda. Sorry. Thanks for the message.'

'Oh, and Rafael sent me a text saying the road east to Argentina is opening soon too, so we can start hikes over that side of the park from tomorrow.'

'Great. Thanks, again. See you later.'

Nacho left his room and went over to the hotel again and up to the guests' rooms. On the way, he met Mrs Towers. She seemed to be sober this time. To Nacho's relief, she made no mention of their last encounter.

'Ah, Señora, can I ask you a quick question? Did your husband like spicy food?' he asked the widow.

'What a strange question. Yes, as a matter of fact he did, or at least he pretended to. Always ate Tex-Mex if it was on the menu. He loved to show off by spooning the hottest salsa on his tacos and adding gallons of Tabasco sauce to Bloody Marys at our rallies and cook-offs back home. He thought it made him look macho. I thought it made him look like a jerk. Why'd you ask?'

'I'm still trying to figure out how he died. Was he poisoned or did some extra hot food stress his body so much that he had a heart attack?'

'I doubt any spicy food would kill off Dwayne. He loved crunching jalapeños straight out of the jar.'

'Thanks for your time, Mrs Towers.'

He left the widow and went and knocked on his targeted door. There was no reply. Using his master key card, he entered his suspect's room. A quick search found what he was looking for. He went to reception once more and, after a few key strokes, the desk clerk revealed the present whereabouts of the person Nacho wanted to see. The wind had dropped temporarily and the sun had come out; it was turning out to be a beautiful day.

CHAPTER 17

Nacho searched the interior of the spa, but the men's changing rooms, the pool, and the massage cubicles were all empty. He went out onto the broad, bleached, wooden sundeck which overhung the turquoise, fast-flowing Rio Paine below. Nacho finally saw the person he was searching for. His suspect was dressed in a white towelling robe and was leaning against the wooden barrier of the balcony, face turned towards the sun, aviator sunglasses covering his eyes.

'Mr Sullivan, I need to talk to you.'

'Ah, Inspector Hernández, how can I help you?' asked the Australian.

'I'm afraid I have evidence that you're a criminal, Mr Sullivan.'

'That's true,' said Sullivan, smiling.

'So, you admit it?'

'Sure. I come from a long line of criminals. That's why one of my ancestors was transported from Ireland to Australia back in the late eighteenth century. "First Fleet" and all that. So, yes, you might say I'm of criminal stock. It's a mark of pride amongst Australians.'

'No, that's not what I meant. I meant that I know you murdered Senator Dwayne Towers.'

'Really? And how did I do that?' asked Sullivan, sounding

surprised. 'I didn't even know Towers was supposed to be here. Nobody did.'

'I believe that you were in the hotel foyer waiting to go out on the Alto del Toro hike with your guide for the day, Miguel, when Senator Towers arrived. He'd been flown into the park by helicopter early that morning and was checking in at reception as your hiking group assembled. You'd therefore have known about his arrival before you set off. You'd also have heard him book the Valle del Francés walk for the next day.'

'Sure, I was in reception then, as you say. Lots of people saw me.'

'I then believe you used the time on your hike with Miguel to figure out a way to kill Towers. Then, at your lunch break that day, you saw Miguel pass out soup and circulate a salt cellar filled with a mix of red chilli powder and salt. You have fast hands, I'm told. I think you stole Miguel's salt cellar and, when you returned from your Alto del Toro hike, you booked Valle del Francés for the next day. You see, I've been told that you're a bit of an amateur magician, Mr Sullivan. The other night in the bar you entertained some of the other guests with some conjuring tricks.'

'You're right, I did do a few tricks the other night. One Christmas, when I was a kid, I asked Santa Claus for a magic set. He delivered, and I loved it! I practised a lot and got quite good at card tricks and other stuff. But what's a salt cellar got to do with a murder?' asked Sullivan, removing his sunglasses and staring at Nacho, his earlier levity having disappeared.

'I think you filled your stolen salt cellar with a mix of pink salt, probably taken from the dining room, and a poison that you had in your luggage – a red powder amongst the various medicines given to you by some aboriginal friends. This red powder, in fact,' said Nacho holding up a small transparent plastic bag that he'd taken from Sullivan's medicine chest. 'I'll have to have this tested by our laboratories, but I'm pretty sure it will correlate to the poison in Towers' body when his autopsy is completed.'

'And what am I supposed to have done with it?'

'I think that, knowing the lunchtime routine, you made sure that you sat beside Towers the next day, when you stopped to eat. He'd have been happy with that, as he'd have known that most of his fellow countrymen and women on the hike didn't like him. Your guide, Hugo, then went through the same ritual as Miguel the day before. He passed out the soup and then circulated the chilli-salt. When the salt got to you, with your conjuring skills you made Hugo's salt pot disappear and passed on Miguel's, your doctored one, to Towers. Apparently, Towers liked to show off how macho he was to his electorate. It was one of his party tricks, so he took a good dose of your chilli-salt and a few minutes later was stricken.'

'And how did you figure all that out?'

'The salt pot here is the one Hugo brought back from the fateful hike,' said Nacho producing Miguel's salt cellar. 'It has a number 7 on its base. Miguel is a big fan of a football player who uses that number. Hugo always used salt pot number 10, his lucky number. There will be no fingerprints on this, I'm sure, as I've checked the photograph of the lunch party and you had thin inner gloves on. Leftover chilli-salt from this pot was left out by Hugo on a stone used to create an artificial salt lick for the local wild animals. Unfortunately, one of the local deer must have enjoyed licking the salt early this morning. It was found dead shortly afterwards. I'm sure an autopsy on it will reveal the same poison as that which killed Towers.'

'And why would I have murdered Senator Towers?' asked Sullivan, who, to Nacho's surprise, had remained surprisingly calm through the litany of accusations.

'At first, I believed you'd killed him because he stood against everything you believe in. A sort of extreme act of protest. You believe that mines should be turned into national parks, whereas he believed national parks should be turned into mines. You believe in climate change and renewable energy, whereas he believed in fossil fuels and was a climate-change denier. You promote women's rights and he was a bit of misogynist and probably guilty of multiple sexual assaults. You're keen on indigenous peoples' rights, whereas Towers was a known anti-immigration racist.'

'That's quite a charge sheet you just laid out there against Towers, Inspector. However, based on that, there are lots of politicians I could have assassinated, not just from America, but from Australia, too. And other places, I dare say. You said "at first". So, I presume you have another motive for me doing this?'

'Yes, I do. I believe it was an act of revenge.'

'Revenge? Revenge for what?'

'Revenge for him shooting down your bomber in the Vietnam War and killing two of your crew. You have a picture in your room of you and two others in front of a Canberra bomber with a caption saying it was taken at a place called Phan Rang. I looked it up. It's in Vietnam.'

'Again true, I did serve in Vietnam,' said Sullivan, but this time his expression was more serious and, for a moment, it looked like his mind was elsewhere.

'I was also told the other day in passing, that Senator Towers had been accused of shooting down an aircraft in a friendly-fire incident back in 1970. I looked that up, too, in the American press. I couldn't find anything about it in *The Washington Post, The New York Times* or *The Washington Recorder*. Nothing. However, in my search, a link came up from a paper called *The Age*, which, as I'm sure you well know, is an Australian daily. In it, there was an article about a Flight Lieutenant Sullivan accusing a USAF pilot of shooting down his bomber. The American pilot was named as Captain Towers. However, Towers' US Air Force commanders and his government supported him and the Australian pilot was sent home.'

'It's amazing what you can find out on the Internet these days, Inspector. So much fake news,' said Sullivan, his face now deadpan.

'So, I think you've borne a grudge against Towers for all this time,' continued Nacho, 'and when he turned up here out of the blue, you took the opportunity to get your revenge on him at last after nearly fifty years. And so, you did as I said. You poisoned him on a hike in plain sight of witnesses who couldn't see how it was done.'

'And how are you going to prove all that, Inspector? Seems to me there are a lot of "ifs, buts, and maybes" in your conjecture. You don't have my fingerprints on the salt pot, you don't have a witness who saw me tampering with the pot or swapping it over, and anyone could have stolen some of that red powder from my room. A maid, a porter, room service, management. All of them with pass keys, just like you, a detective who could have planted it there to conveniently solve his crime.'

'You're right, Mr Sullivan. Little of what I've said would stand up in court, especially in front of a good lawyer defending a major benefactor of the Chilean economy and its environmental future. And in any case, I haven't informed a prosecutor of my findings, and, if and when I do, they might throw my case out. So, you see, Mr Sullivan, you're pretty safe for now. I just want to know if I'm right.'

Sullivan looked at Nacho for a long time and then broke into a smile.

'Well done, Inspector, you've pretty much sussed out my modus operandi. I've hated Towers ever since he shot down my Canberra almost fifty years ago to the day. He was piloting an F-4 Phantom on a CAP. That's a Combat Air Patrol. It was north of our airbase. He hit us with a Sidewinder heat-seeking missile as we were coming back to Phan Rang. I managed to eject, but my two crew didn't get out and were killed. As I floated down, I could see an F-4 circling us, before heading off to its own base, and so I knew it had to be the one who intercepted us. Of course, at the time, I didn't know it was Towers, just some American fighter jock, as the US were the only Phantom operators in Vietnam. A US Army patrol saw me come down and radioed for a Huey helicopter to come and pick me up. As we lifted off, I could see the wreck on my Canberra burning in a paddy field. My two crew must have been still inside,' said Sullivan, and then he paused, a faraway look in his eye.

Nacho suspected that, in his mind, the Australian was back in Vietnam. He prompted Sullivan by asking, 'What happened next?'

'Well, when I got back to base and debriefed, I told my superiors what had happened. I could sense right away that they thought I'd been mistaken and that I must have been hit by a Mig or a SAM missile. There were no Migs or SAMs operating that far south, but they obviously didn't want to upset our Allies, especially since we were actually hosted within an American fighter wing.'

'So, how did you find out it was Towers?'

'I did a little investigating on my own. I found out which USAF squadron was on CAP duty that day, took a jeep, and went up to their base. I questioned a few officers there and found out that one of their pilots, a Captain Towers, had just been declared an "ace" after shooting down a "Beagle".'

'A beagle? What do you mean, a beagle?' asked Nacho, confused. The only beagle he knew was a type of dog, although it was also the title of a channel full of fjords off Tierra del Fuego, named after a British ship from olden times.

'An Ilyushin Il-28. A Russian-made bomber with the NATO type codename of "Beagle". The North Vietnamese had a few of them. Although it had two engines like my Canberra, they were mounted under the wing, unlike ours, and the wing was on the fuselage shoulder, unlike ours, and it had a tail gunner position, and we didn't. Any fighter pilot worth their salt should have noticed all those physical differences, never mind the fact that our camouflage scheme was different to the North Vietnamese, and that we had bloody big blue roundel markings with a red kangaroo in the middle on our wings. A decent American pilot would have known that Canberras were not only being used by their Australian allies, but even their own air force.'

'What did the Americans say?'

'As soon as I made my claim that I'd been shot down by this Towers bloke, the Yanks all clammed up. Said I must be mistaken. Towers was the son of a US congressman and now he was an ace and a bona fide hero. One of their NCOs though, who thought Towers was a pain in the ass because he treated the enlisted men badly, let me know that Towers had gone down to Saigon to celebrate becoming an ace and to give press interviews.'

'Saigon?'

'Ho Chi Minh City, as it is now. The commies renamed it for their leader after they won the war. So, anyway, I went down to Saigon and did the rounds of the bars and clubs the Air Force officers preferred, and eventually I tracked Towers down. He was drinking with his navigator and some of his squadron buddies. I'd had a few drinks myself along the way, and I was fighting mad. I strode up to his table and accused him of killing my mates, but he just blew me off. When I went to take a swing at him, some of his friends pulled me away and chucked me out. I hung around outside the toilets and when his navigator came over to use the john, I accosted him. The guy was pretty drunk by then and admitted to me that he'd told Towers our aircraft was probably a Martin B-57 – that's American for a Canberra. Towers ignored him and launched a Sidewinder anyway. Just as I was getting more of the story, and got the navigator to agree to testify about what he'd told me, I noticed Towers was beside us. He'd heard the last part of his nav's confession and pulled him away from me. He whistled up some MP goons and told them I was harassing him, and I was taken away from the club.'

'So, what did you do next?' asked Nacho, engrossed in the story unfolding.

'I later found out, that on his way back to his billet that night, Towers had been involved in a road traffic accident. The jeep he was in crashed and, while his navigator was killed, Towers was only roughed up a bit. Now, coincidence or what? Well, I'm like an old dog with a bone, Inspector. I went out to the scene of the crash the next day. Sure enough, there was a jeep, nose down in a drainage ditch. I asked around in a nearby village and found one old guy who claimed he'd seen the crash the night before. He said the jeep had stopped and the driver had got out, but there was a passenger asleep in the front. The old guy claimed the driver twisted the neck of the passenger, moved him into the driver's seat, and then pushed the jeep into the ditch.'

'So, you think Towers was a murderer, too? Why wasn't he charged?'

'Exactly. So, I got some USAF Police to come out and see my witness. Just as we got there, we saw a jeep leaving the other side of the village. Then, my witness denied everything he'd told me. Strangely, there was a brand-new Kawasaki sitting outside the old guy's house and a set of matching keys on his table. The guy was dirt poor, so how was he suddenly the proud owner of a new bike?'

'You think Towers got wind of your accusation and bought him off with a motorbike?'

'That's exactly what I think. I think someone in the police warned him of my inquiries and witness. At the end of the day, it was officially assumed that it was the nav that was drunk behind the wheel, as it couldn't possibly be a war hero and fighter ace, could it?'

'So, I was right, after all these years, the injustice around your colleagues still clearly burned inside you, and you added Towers' own crewman to your list of his victims?' asked Nacho.

'Colleagues? Colleagues? These were mates, Inspector,' said Sullivan, his voice rising. 'Mateship is a religion in Australia, especially in war. Has been since Gallipoli, over a hundred years ago. And these weren't ordinary mates, Inspector. Johnny, my navigator, was the best man at my wedding and my wife's brother to boot. Phil, my bomb aimer, had a pregnant wife back in Oz who was my wife, Jenny's, best friend. Towers was a spineless bastard who couldn't own up to his own mistake. I tried to pursue him through our high command, but that didn't work. They weren't interested, or at least accepted that these things happen in war. I then tried the press, and that didn't work either. I was sent home. Eventually, I had to focus on my family and my business, but I never forgot about Towers, and I swore to myself that if I ever got the opportunity, I would take the bastard down for good.'

Sullivan paused in his story. He took a few deep breaths, then shook his head, and continued.

'I kept track of Towers and all his political antics over the years. It's not difficult these days with the Internet and access to news channels from across the globe. It was clear that as my own thoughts over time became more liberal and I became environmentally aware, Towers seemed to go in the opposite direction to ensure his re-election by his base of poorly-educated and disaffected voters. I began to not just hate the man for what he'd done to Johnny and Phil, but to despise him for his beliefs, too.

'Then the other day, who should walk into this hotel, completely unexpected, but none other than Senator Dwayne Towers. I couldn't believe my eyes at first. Then it sunk in. Here was my opportunity. So, I crystallised my plan. I stole Miguel's salt pot and doctored it as you've described, steered Towers to the edge of the group at lunch on Hugo's hike so he'd get the doctored salt after me with no collateral damage of a second death, and then fed him the chilli-salt. As I've said, he was a macho type of guy, so he added a big dose of it to his soup to show the others what a strong man he was. And so, after fifty years, I got my revenge and rid the world of this despicable human being.'

'A human being, nonetheless, Mr Sullivan, and what you did was commit murder. Did you not think about your reputation if your crime was discovered?'

'It really doesn't matter to me, Inspector. You see, after my daughter died, and then when my wife succumbed to breast cancer a few years later, I'd little to live for other than trying to leave the world a better place, set for a cleaner future. Then I found out I had a brain tumour.'

'You don't act like a man with a brain tumour, Mr Sullivan.'

'It's a slow-growing type called "Oligodendroglioma". At least I think that's what it's called. Hell of a name and hell of a thing not to know what's killing you, don't you think?' said Sullivan, backed by a short laugh.

'I'm sorry to hear that, Mr Sullivan,' said Nacho, wondering if it was true as the man in front of him seemed quite healthy.

'It's slow growing and was probably there for years before the doctors detected it. I get headaches and occasional seizures, but it will eventually kill me. So, you see, Inspector, I know I'm going to die shortly anyway. Some of my friends from our indigenous peoples gave me a medicine chest with their native medicines. They help the pain and reduce the convulsions, but they also gave me a powder – the one you have in your hand – in case I found it all too much and wanted to end my life. So, you're right in how I did it, and I ended Towers' life instead of mine. Oh, look, the cloud's clearing from the Cuernos,' said Sullivan, suddenly changing tack, and pointing behind Nacho at the skyline.

Instinctively, Nacho turned around and indeed the Paine Massif was once more resplendent in a cloudless sky, its craggy features accentuated by the shadows cast by the low sunshine. When Nacho turned back to Sullivan, he found the Australian had stepped over the barrier and was now standing on the edge of the balcony, inches away from the abyss below and its raging torrent.

'What are you doing, Mr Sullivan? Please, come back over here.'

'I don't think so, Inspector. Better all round if I have an accident, don't you think? No damage to my legacy, as you said. Chile will eventually get new national parks, the indigenous peoples will inherit my fortune, and I'll avoid the expected pain of my tumour growing to its terminal state.'

Sullivan took a transparent plastic bag like the one in Nacho's hand out of the pocket of his robe and then said, 'This here yellow powder is the one indigenous folks use to stun fish. They put it in the water, and the fish ingests it and then floats on the surface for easy capture. I've used a little of it at a time to control my convulsions. If I use a lot, I dare say I won't be able to swim or feel a thing as I drown.' Sullivan emptied the bag's contents into his mouth and then stepped backwards, falling ten metres into the Rio Paine below, too quick in his actions for Nacho to grab him.

'Help! Man in the water, man in the water,' yelled Nacho, looking around for a life preserver.

By the time he found a lifebelt, he could see Sullivan's body floating rapidly down the river. Nacho called the Ranger HQ to scramble a car and a boat from downriver to see if they could rescue Sullivan. However, he suspected that the man was already dead from drowning or the shock of falling into the permanently cold waters of the Rio Paine. He ran to the parking area and jumped in his Land Rover. He raced down the road parallel to the river. Nacho arrived at the Explora Hotel's walkway just as Sullivan's body disappeared in the raging froth of the Salto Chico waterfall. The body reappeared moments later, stripped of its robe, and continued its naked voyage towards Lago Toro. Nacho got back in his vehicle and pursued the body. He knew it had come to rest when he noticed a pair of condors circling above the Puente Weber Bridge. The giant carrion-eaters were a sure sign that something was dead below their aerobatic gyre.

Sullivan's body was eventually picked up by rangers in a boat. It had snagged on one of the piers underneath the bridge. The body was brought ashore, and Nacho put it in his Land Rover and drove it back to the Último. The maintenance crew and rangers helped him prepare a coffin for the old Australian and it was placed beside the body of Senator Towers in the hotel's cold store. The irony of the two lying side by side in death wasn't lost on Nacho as he closed the refrigerator door.

In the short period before Captain Figueroa arrived, Nacho had Hugo pack and drive off on the reopened road to Cerro Castillo where he could cross the border into Argentina. He ensured that Hugo would be let through in a call back to his police headquarters in Puerto Natales. In the call he was also told that two Colombian citizens had been detained. The men had been found in possession of firearms, masks, and maps marked with possible ambush sites.

Nacho then called the DG in Santiago on his unlisted number using Fernanda's mobile and told him about his suspicions regarding Mr Sullivan and his subsequent conversation with the Australian. Finally, he told the DG about Sullivan's suicide. At the end of their conversation, the DG said he would phone Nacho back shortly.

About half an hour later Nacho's own mobile rang as he stood at the hotel's picture window, looking out onto the massif once more, his thoughts with the dead Australian. It was the DG again, obviously comfortable that the message he was now about to relay to Nacho could be heard by the ANI.

'I've had a discussion with the Minister of the Interior and Public Security. He in turn has talked to both the Australian and American Embassies. Urgent diplomatic cables have been exchanged between Santiago, Canberra and Washington. The official line will be that Senator Towers died of a heart attack while on a short vacation after a successful fact-finding trip to Chile. This will be confirmed from his autopsy by a high-ranking government pathologist under an American observer. A Chilean communiqué will recognise that, due to Senator Towers' unselfish efforts, the United States has agreed to sell Chile additional F-16 fighters for its Air Force inventory. The US government will stress the Senator's track record as a long-serving senator, war hero, and champion of his selected causes. The impression our minister got was that the White House wasn't too upset as Towers was seen lately as taking too much of the political limelight away from the President.

'I also understand that the Senator's wife will be bought off by his party guaranteeing her the succession for his safe seat in the Senate. Towers will be given a nice funeral at Arlington National Cemetery to keep his friends and his political base happy. I think it's believed that if the story came out as to why Towers was actually murdered, his whole record, some of which is not too pleasant, will be raked over by the press, damaging his party and potentially the President in an election year.'

'But what about his friend here, that imbecile, Dawson?'

'His friend will be leaned on to fall into line. I gather he'll be near the top of the queue for oil concessions when the US government opens up new areas of Alaska. Money talks for the Dawsons of this world. I take it from your tone and descriptor that you're not keen on the man? Well, I'm not either, so Mr Dawson may experience a little difficulty with our customs and passport control officers as he tries to exit the country. He'll miss his flight. Such a shame.'

Nacho smiled when he heard this news, and then asked, 'And what about the journalist, Zinczenko, sir?'

'Mr Zinczenko will be reinstated in his old job now Towers is gone, as long as he admits his initial suspicions regarding the Senator's death were unproven.'

'And Sullivan? What will be said about him?'

'Regarding Mr Sullivan, it will be revealed that he was suffering from a severe illness, and that he took his own life in a sort of euthanasia gesture to save himself months or even years of pain. His death is therefore completely unconnected to that of Senator Towers. Our government will say that Jim Sullivan was a great friend of Chile who had invested billions of dollars in mines to produce the minerals needed for the green electrification of, not only Chile, but the world. His legacy will be further enhanced upon the rehabilitation of his mine sites in Chile into national parks at a future date. The Australians will make the most of his philanthropic gesture of leaving his company to their indigenous peoples and the appointment of a female CEO as his replacement.

'In other words, Hernández, everybody will be happy. All three governments have an acceptable outcome, Towers' widow becomes a senator, the Último Hotel and this TripLux tour operator are in the clear, and even you come out of this well – in police circles at least. You solved the case, even if no perpetrator will be punished. Now, given what I've just said, you must of course keep the real version of events confidential, and I'm sure that if you do, you will soon be back here in Santiago.'

'Right, sir, I get it,' said Nacho, understanding only too well the carrot and stick in the DG's message.

'Captain Figueroa and his FBI attendants will be told the same thing. Someone is speaking to them right now, even as I speak to you. They will follow the same official line.'

'Thank you, sir. I've got a few loose ends to tie up here, so I may have to stay on one more day, if that's okay, sir?'

'Fine, I'll square it with your chief. Oh, and Hernández?'

'Yes, sir?'

'Well done.'

As Nacho terminated the call, he heard a lot of car-door slamming occurring outside. He went out to look and found two black Chevrolet Suburbans depositing a bunch of crew-cut, sunglass-wearing, male thirty-somethings on to the hotel driveway. A bald older man got out of a green and white Carabineros Dodge Durango. Captain Figueroa, Nacho presumed.

Behind the police convoy, a set of large aluminium cases stood beside a grey Ford van. A technician was assembling a portable satellite dish, while a cameraman and sound engineer stood before a reporter who was already doing a piece to camera about their arrival at the Último Hotel, scene of Senator Towers' death, and their exclusive access to the breaking story.

Nacho went across to greet Figueroa. He was glad that he had solved the case before these heavies and the TV crew had arrived, and, even if Sullivan was a murderer, he was also glad that the Australian had taken his own way out. Nacho found that he was not particularly concerned that Senator Towers had died, as everything that he'd learned about the man, a possible murderer himself, made it difficult to be overly upset by his demise. It was no way for a policeman to think. "Must do better", as his old school teacher used to say.

After talking to the captain, Nacho sought out the Morgans, and asked to talk to his erstwhile pathologist on her own.

'I'm sorry to have to tell you, Dr Morgan, but it has been decided that Senator Towers did indeed die of a heart attack after all.'

'Really, Inspector?' queried the doctor, a surprised look on her face.

'Yes, it was brought on by political expediency, if you get what I mean.'

'Ah, I get your drift. This would be the best solution for everyone involved, I take it?'

'Exactly. Best for Chile, America and Australia.'

'Australia, too? Well, well, then yes, I do see your point, Inspector. Mum's the word.'

'You've used that expression before, Doctor, and I don't understand it. I know a lot of English idioms, but not that one. Whose mum, or even who is Mum?'

The doctor laughed and explained, 'It's an old English expression. "Mum" in this case means to keep quiet. We had silent actors called "mummers", you know, like Pierrots or mime artists, if you like. It means "I won't say a word".'

'Thank you, Doctor, and thanks again too, for all your help.'

'Not a problem, Inspector. It made my little trip here a bit more exciting. While the scenery is truly wonderful, having a geologist for a husband does take the shine off it a bit. Alwyn is always banging on about biotite, sillimanite, kyanite and all sorts of other "ites" in his beloved hornfels, so your little investigation was a welcome diversion, believe me.'

Nacho and the doctor shook hands and she went off to rejoin her husband. As he watched her go, Nacho thought, not for the first time, that despite his fluency, British understatement and the richness of the English language would never cease to surprise him. As his old English teacher used to say, "Why have only one word for something to confuse foreigners, when you can have twenty, gathered from the Romans, an empire, allies and enemies, invaders, and traders?".

Next, Nacho went looking for the journalist who had started the whole investigation into the "suspicious circumstances" around Senator Towers' death. He found Zinczenko in the bar.

'Good afternoon, Inspector. Come and join me. I'm celebrating with a few Pisco Sours.'

'What are you celebrating, Señor?'

'I've just put the phone down on my old editor at *The Washington Recorder*. He's offered me my old job back. He said I could hang my shingle outside his door if I confirmed that Dwayne Towers died of a heart attack. Did he?'

'That depends,' said Nacho in reply.

'Depends on what?'

'Depends on whether you want your job back or not?'

'Hmm. I'll take that as a "no", but I do want my job back. Even with a bombastic piece of shit like Towers gone, there's plenty of other rotting fish in the Washington market to gut and grill. Not to mention that I've alimony payments to make, kids to put through college, a mortgage to pay, and other sundry expenses. So, I guess I'll withdraw my tweet about "suspicious circumstances" around the death of the old bastard. "Needs must, when the Devil drives", and all that jazz.'

'That sounds the right way to go.'

'Uh huh. And I heard we've had another death here at the hotel. Some Aussie billionaire. Any story there? Any "suspicious circumstances"?'

'That story's already been told.'

'What story?'

'Look up back copies of *The Age*, the Australian newspaper. You might find it has a fishy story from the past involving a cover-up from fifty years ago. However, if you retell it, it may cost you your job all over again.'

Zinczenko looked hard at Nacho, smiled, and then asked, 'Vietnam? Thanks for the tip. I'll look it up, Inspector, and then decide.'

'Tip? It's more than my job's worth to give an investigative journalist a tip, Mr Zinczenko, you know that,' said Nacho, mirroring the journalist's smile.

'Sure. I'll keep your name out of it. Thanks.'

'Good hunting, Mr Zinczenko, and goodbye.'

CHAPTER 18

After one more night together, Nacho and Fernanda drove off early the next day through the park, to Ascencio in the east. It was still dark when they parked the Land Rover, added some extra layers of clothing, put on head torches, hitched up their rucksacks, and hit the Valle Ascencio trail. After an hour and a half of hiking, they reached a small glacial lake. The last part of their journey had been particularly dangerous in the dark, as they'd clambered over a boulder field in fierce winds. They found they were alone at their chosen spot and they sat down, shared a flask of coffee, ate energy bars, and stared out north-west into the dark. They held hands, and then held their breath, as one of the world's great light shows materialised in front of them, powered by the rising sun behind them.

As the gloom slowly lightened, a rockface was revealed across the lake, and then, above it, appeared the three iconic rock towers – the eponymous Torres del Paine. The three tall columns of granite with their jagged tops turned deeper shades of pink before their eyes. It was truly stunning. Even though both had seen the view before, they still sat there in silence, mesmerized by the magical sight, enjoying the moment together. Eventually the spell was broken as the sun rose higher, the pink hue disappeared, and a number of other hikers arrived.

They drove back to the Último and Fernanda got out of the Land Rover after kissing Nacho farewell.

'Will I see you in Puerto Natales soon?' asked Nacho through his wound-down window.

'We'll see. I'll think about it.'

'Don't think too hard,' said Nacho and Fernanda laughed. 'But anyway, I may be back here sooner rather than later.'

'Really? To see me or another sunrise?'

'Both are equally beautiful.'

'Why, Nacho, you're a poet!'

'I've been called many things before, but never a poet.'

'Well, write me a love poem and, if I like it, I'll come to Puerto Natales.'

'In that case, look at your email tonight. It's a long drive back and I'll compose something on the way. How could I not be inspired by what I've seen this morning and what I enjoyed last night?'

'I look forward to it. I'll have my very own Pablo Neruda.'

'Well, it may not be up to his standards, so don't judge me too harshly.'

'I won't. Now I've got to go and say goodbye to our TripLux guests. They're leaving soon. Drive safely. Text me that you're back okay.'

Nacho drove out of the hotel gate, his mind already turning to words that rhymed with "Torres del Paine".

ACKNOWLEDGEMENTS

My thanks to the following for their advice and encouragement:
Janet Walker, Rachel Wilkinson, Nichola Kolsaker, Kristian Kolsaker, Matthew Wilkinson, Nick Thripp, and Rachel Marsh.

ALSO BY DAVID D WALKER

BLACKMAIL

Blackmail-Erpressung-Chantage – English-German-French – actors
from all three countries engage in a web of blackmail behind the
lines in 1916 that Captain Jamie Brown has to unravel in case the
"Big Push" (the Somme offensive) is compromised and a royal sex
scandal exposed. He has to deal with recognisable modern themes of
injudicial killing, gay rights, fake news, kompromat, and organised
crime in a First World War context. Jamie finds himself on a personal
journey that questions his own beliefs and his ability to control his
nerves and his drinking, as he deals with his own country's deep state,
a fractious ally, and an enemy master spy. Along the way he has to
cope with snipers, air aces, spies, gangsters, corrupt policemen, and
prostitutes – all woven into the blackmail web.

Blackmail is also published by Matador/Troubador.

ABOUT THE AUTHOR

David Walker is a retired executive who turned to writing late in life. He is a keen amateur historian and global traveller. He was born in Hamilton, Scotland, and studied geology at Edinburgh University and Imperial College, before embarking on an international career in the energy industry. He has lived in the USA, Norway, and the Netherlands. He now resides in Guildford, Surrey, with his wife.

 Matador

For exclusive discounts on Matador titles,
sign up to our occasional newsletter at
troubador.co.uk/bookshop